TH

An epic series of frontier survival and family spirit by award-winning author Gary McCarthy

The Horsemen

The Ballous were the finest horsemen in the South. But as the Civil War raged, they left Tennessee—to face unimaginable hardship, danger, and ruthless enemies . . .

Cherokee Lighthorse

Houston, Ruff, and Dixie Ballou intend to survive together in the West. But there are deserters wandering the roads who would kill for their horses—and others who would kill them just for being Southern . . .

Texas Mustangers

In Texas, the Ballous discovered a tribe of Indians who shared their love and respect for horses—and another tribe who offered a deadly challenge to anyone foolish enough to cross their path . . .

Blue Bullet

The Ballous must accept a challenge to capture Blue Bullet—the legendary stallion that no man has been able to tame. But the proud horse is hunted by others as well—savage killers who will bring in their bounty dead or alive . . .

THE HORSEMEN

STALLION VALLEY

GARY McCARTHY

JOVE BOOKS, NEW YORK

STALLION VALLEY

A Jove Book / published by arrangement with
the author

PRINTING HISTORY
Jove edition / August 1994

ISBN: 0-515-11434-0

A JOVE BOOK®
Jove Books are published by The Berkley Publishing Group,
200 Madison Avenue, New York, New York 10016.
JOVE and the "J" design are trademarks
belonging to Jove Publications, Inc.

PRINTED IN THE UNITED STATES OF AMERICA

10 9 8 7 6 5 4 3 2 1

ONE

Rufus "Ruff" Ballou and his fifteen-year-old sister, Dixie, reined in their handsome Thoroughbred stallions to let them drink their fill in the Rio Grande.

"My oh my," Ruff said, thumbing back his Stetson and taking a long, admiring look at the huge and grassy valley that bordered the Rio Grande. "Is this pretty country, or have we died and found paradise?"

Dixie's brown eyes tracked across the high mountain valley located in northeastern New Mexico. The grass was long and nutritious, and she liked the spectacular backdrop of the towering Sangre de Cristo Mountains with their snowcapped peaks. "It is beautiful. In fact, I've never seen a more picturesque valley."

Ruff glanced over at the exceptional band of sixteen Thoroughbred brood mares they were trailing north toward Denver. "Dixie, what would you think about buying some of this valley land and building our horse ranch right here?"

"My only concern is the altitude. I'm afraid that this country is a little high," Dixie said. "We must be well over seven thousand feet, and I'll bet the snow gets ten feet deep in the winter."

Ruff had already thought of that and had a solution. "In the winter, we could trail our horses down to Santa Fe or to the even milder Albuquerque, both of which have plenty of racing horses and tracks. And in the summer and fall, we could race at Taos, which isn't very far north."

Dixie frowned. "I thought we were on our way to Colorado."

"Denver is also high," Ruff argued. "And I doubt that it's any prettier. Besides, other than Denver, I haven't heard of any towns with horse racing opportunities to match Albuquerque, Santa Fe, or Taos. I'm telling you, Dixie, I think this is where we ought to buy land and put down our roots."

"And what do you propose using for money?"

"We've got a few hundred dollars."

"Not nearly enough."

"Then we can sell a couple of our purebred mares. Every last one of them is worth at least five hundred dollars."

"In Tennessee or the Kentucky bluegrass country where we come from they're worth that much, but not here in New Mexico."

"I don't know about that."

"I do. We've been out west long enough to know that ranchers look at our tall, long-legged horses and are sure that they won't stand up to hard use."

Ruff had to admit this was true. He affectionately scratched his young stallion's neck. "I'd match High Fire or old High Man against anything the cowboys ride in this New Mexico country."

"Of course you would," Dixie said. "These stallions have proven themselves on the track, and they've never failed us since we left Wildwood Farm. Our father would have been proud of the way his Thoroughbreds have adapted to the West."

Ruff looked away with pain mirrored in his eyes when he thought about what little remained of his once prominent Tennessee horse-raising family. It had been almost eighteen months since General Grant's Union armies had driven into the South and destroyed the famed Tennessee Ballou horse ranch named Wildwood Farm. Ruff and Dixie had earlier lost their two eldest brothers on Civil War battlefields, and their father had died attempting to keep the very last of their prized horses from being confiscated by a ruthless Confederate officer. And there was no way of telling if their brother, Houston Ballou, was alive or dead, because he had fallen in love and gone north in search of a brave Confederate spy by the name of Molly O'Day. Ruff had a bad feeling that Houston was already dead, either shot, or hanged as a spy.

"There is supposed to be a town just a few more miles up ahead," Dixie said. "Why don't we spend the night there and see if we can find buyers for a mare or two, then ask about local land prices? This entire valley might already be claimed."

"I'm sure that it is," Ruff said. "But there are bound to be a few bargain-priced homesteads for sale."

"I wouldn't count on that."

But Ruff wasn't concerned. Their family's Tennessee horse farm had been less than 160 acres, and that had been sufficient to raise more than fifty prized Thoroughbreds with paddocks and pastures aplenty. Perhaps in this country a man might need a little more ground, but it was only April and the grass and wild oats were already knee-high. Local farmers and ranchers would get one cutting, maybe even two, of grass hay.

"Dixie, if we settle here, I'd want to build up against the pine trees and high enough above this river so that we wouldn't have to worry about flooding."

"I haven't seen any sign of it this spring," Dixie said. "And they had a heavy winter snowfall."

"That's true," Ruff admitted, "but when you are surrounded by mountains, you'd better be concerned about spring runoff and flooding."

"I suppose you are right."

High Fire raised his head to signal that he'd had his fill of water. His father, High Man, and their band of Thoroughbred mares did the same. Ruff lifted his reins. "Let's push on and find out what land sells for in these parts."

"If the prices are based on the scenery," Dixie warned, "they'll be as high as these mountain peaks."

Ruff was about to say something when four men galloped into view. Even at a distance, Ruff could hear their horses' labored breathing and see that the animals were flecked with foam.

"Those men are running from some kind of trouble," Ruff said. "And if they don't give their horses a breather, they're gonna kill 'em."

Dixie agreed. The four riders were furiously whipping and spurring their mounts. Just watching them made Dixie's blood boil, for she could not abide the mistreatment of animals, especially horses. Ruff, she knew, felt exactly the same way. Their late and beloved father, Justin Ballou, had always taught them that you could get more out of an animal—any animal—with kindness rather than force. Most men didn't believe that, but that only proved that they were ignorant.

"They're coming right for us," Ruff said with mounting anxiety. "We'd better drive our mares out of the way or these fools will scatter them to hell and back."

But before Ruff and Dixie could get themselves and their horses out of the approaching danger, the four men were charging through them, cursing and shouting. One of the men spurred his flagging mount into High Man. The old

Thoroughbred staggered, almost unseating Dixie. It made Ruff so furious that he put his heels to the flanks of High Fire and sent the stallion racing after the man.

High Fire overtook his prey in less than twenty yards, and when Ruff drew even, he shouted, "What the hell is the matter with you fellas!"

The man glanced sideways in surprise and went for his six-gun. Ruff was good with a six-gun and fast, but he was so shocked by this man's reaction that there wasn't time to reach for his own Colt. Instead, he smashed the rider in the jaw, knocking him completely out of the saddle. The crazy fool landed on his head, and Ruff heard the sickening crack of a broken neck. The man's horse raced on to catch up with its companions.

The other three riders were a hundred yards farther on when the riderless horse joined them. They twisted around in their saddles, saw their companion was down, and reined to a halt.

"Uh-oh," Ruff said to himself as the three riders came charging back, dragging guns from their holsters. Ruff wheeled High Fire away from the river and yelled, "Dixie, round up our mares and get out of here!"

"No!" she screamed, jumping off their old foundation stallion and grabbing a saddle carbine which she could use better than most men.

The three riders unleashed a wild volley at fifty yards, and by then, Ruff had also dismounted and sent his Thoroughbred trotting out of the line of fire. Ruff drew his pistol, took aim, and his shot blended with the heavier retort of Dixie's carbine as two more saddles were emptied. The last rider broke off the charge and went galloping for cover in the pine-dotted foothills.

"I couldn't shoot him in the back," Dixie called, lowering her carbine.

"I wouldn't have expected you to," Ruff said, striding over to examine the three intruders.

Two were dead, but the one that Ruff had shot was still breathing despite a bullet through the lungs. Ruff knelt at the dying man's side. "What the hell kind of a burr did you boys have under your saddles?"

The man's breathing was labored, and crimson froth was seeping from the corner of his mouth. Ruff glanced sideways at Dixie, who shook her head.

"What's your name?" Ruff asked. "Who are your next of kin?"

The man's lips moved and he struggled to speak. Instead, he began to cough and spew more blood. Ruff placed his hand on the man's shoulder. "Just rest easy."

"Tell . . . Jessica that I . . ."

But before the man could give Ruff his complete message, he shivered into death.

Ruff stood up. He was a shade over six-four and tougher than rawhide, with dark brown eyes from the Cherokee side of the Ballou family. "Wonder who Jessica is," he asked aloud, "and what kind of trouble these fellas were running from."

"I have no idea." Dixie looked off toward where the fourth man had disappeared. "I guess the one that got away is the only man that might be able to tell us."

"Maybe I should go after him."

"I think you'd better not. Whoever it is that rode off might be waiting in ambush."

Ruff suspected that his sister was right. "Guess we ought to take these bodies into the next town. Maybe there's a marshal or someone who could explain things."

"I'm not sure that's such a good idea."

"Why not?"

"It just seems to me that, if there really is a possibility that we might buy some land here, this is a bad omen."

"Ahh!" Ruff scoffed. "I don't believe in omens. Besides, we're not the ones that are to blame here. We were attacked and you were almost trampled to death."

"That's right," Dixie said, "but you have to admit that killing three men is a poor introduction to the locals."

"Maybe so, but I sure wish we knew who these men were and why they were running their horses so hard."

"My guess is that they were in some kind of trouble. Maybe they robbed a bank and we'll earn a reward."

"Maybe," Ruff said, sounding doubtful.

"Let's see if they were carrying a lot of cash."

"All right."

Ruff went through their pockets and didn't find much except jackknives and a few crumpled dollars. "Could be the money was in their saddlebags. That's where I'd put it if I robbed a bank."

"Me, too. We ought to look for their runaway horses."

Ruff glanced southward. "I'll ride around that bend in the river and see if I can spot 'em."

"Good idea. But hurry back. This whole thing has me a little spooked."

"I'll be back before you know it," Ruff promised, mounting High Fire and reining off down the river.

His young Thoroughbred stallion was a sorrel with a blaze and white stockings. Ruff had raised and trained the magnificent animal. When High Fire got up a head of steam, there was nothing in the West that could outrun his horse, and now High Fire carried him swiftly down his backtrail along the Rio Grande. The river was running bank to bank, and it looked icy, snow-fed, and treacherous as it roiled down the great Rio Grande Valley toward a distant Albuquerque. Ruff didn't see the riderless horses and decided to push on to the next bend in the river.

But when he rounded it, he wished he'd minded his own business and stayed with Dixie, because, not only did he find the three riderless horses, but he also spotted several heavily armed horsemen who believed in the adage that it was better to shoot first and ask questions later.

When a rifle slug hummed meanly only a few inches overhead, Ruff brought High Fire up to a skidding halt. He whirled the stallion around and took off back upriver to join Dixie, with the men hot on his heels. Riding with extraordinary skill, Ruff was able to increase the distance between himself and his pursuers. When he reached Dixie, he shouted, "Gather the mares and let's run for it!"

Dixie didn't understand until she saw the riders chasing her brother. Then, with no need for further explanation, she drove their Thoroughbred mares hard upriver. Ruff held back to protect his sister and their horses against what he figured were more outlaws or just some common horse thieves. But their pursuers abruptly broke off the chase in order to gather the riderless horses. Minutes later, they disappeared into the foothills. Ruff pulled in High Fire, confused and a little shaken after two shoot-outs in less than ten minutes.

"Dixie, hold up!"

Dixie reined up High Man, and their mares slowed to a ragged trot, nostrils distended and eyes rolling with excitement.

"One thing for sure," Ruff said, shaking his head with confusion. "This is the damnedest country for people shooting at other people that I have ever seen!"

"It's all an unlucky coincidence," Dixie explained. "We've obviously stumbled into the middle of trouble.

Maybe a range war. I don't know. But whatever thinking more and more about Denver City."

"Me, too," Ruff admitted, constantly glancing back ov\ his shoulder. "I just hope that someone finds and buries those three men we shot. Hate to see the animals eat 'em."

Dixie shuddered. "I feel like we've just been caught in a Texas tornado."

They both reloaded their weapons. When Ruff was satisfied that they weren't being chased, he said, "New Mexico is a little too wild for me. Let's get to Colorado."

"That suits me."

So they gathered their band of fine Thoroughbred mares and pushed hard up the Rio Grande Valley, wondering why they had been attacked twice in the space of a very few minutes and how long it would take them to reach a more peaceful Colorado.

TWO

Rio Paso w.   a thriving community that depended on mining, timber, and ranching for its livelihood. One of the very first things that Ruff noticed as they approached the town was that it had a pretty decent racetrack complete with an inside rail and grandstands.

"Looks to me like these people enjoy horse racing," Ruff said to his sister.

He galloped over to the track, judging it to be about a half-mile circuit. The track itself was graded and free of rocks. When Ruff dismounted and scooped up a handful of dirt, he found it to be a fine textured soil that would yield good drainage and footing.

"What do you think?" he asked his young stallion, letting the dirt sift between his fingers. "Looks like good, fast footing. Bet they've never had a horse on this track that can run as fast as you can."

As if understanding the compliment, High Fire bobbed his head in agreement. Ruff remounted and galloped back to join Dixie and their other Thoroughbreds. "Good track," he announced. "It'd be even better with an outside rail, but for a town this size, it's not bad at all."

"What about tonight?" Dixie asked. "Shall we find a livery, or do you just want to camp on the outskirts and save the feed and board bill?"

"Let's camp and save money. The grass is good, and it doesn't make any sense to buy hay."

Dixie nodded with agreement, although she knew they

would both have preferred to board their horses and take a hotel room after a week of camping under the stars.

"I suppose," Dixie said, "you're going to want to be the first one to ride into Rio Paso, while I am stuck guarding our horses."

"That makes sense, doesn't it?" Ruff asked. "I can find the marshal and explain to him what happened with those three jaspers that we were forced to kill in self-defense."

"Are you sure that we shouldn't just keep riding on without creating a stir? There's no telling what those men did before attacking us, and I sure don't want to get all tangled up in their mischief."

"But what if they just robbed a bank and there is a big reward? Don't you even want to cash in on it?"

Dixie was forced to smile. "It never fails, you always look at the bright side."

"And you the dark. I'll just bet you that those four were in trouble and running from the law. I'm thinking that we really might earn a reward."

"That would sure be a pleasant surprise, but I don't think it's very likely."

Ruff shrugged. He pointed toward the Rio Grande. "Let's make our camp down yonder along the river's bank where those cottonwoods will give us protection in case the wind starts to blowing tonight. Those trees will also provide us with a good supply of firewood."

"All right, go into town and explain what happened to their marshal. But before you return, I want you to buy something for us to eat. We're running low on food."

"What sounds good?"

Dixie didn't hesitate. "I'd like you to stop at the butcher shop and buy steaks to roast. And maybe some canned peaches for dessert. Or, if they don't have any peaches, bring back a nice big pie."

"A pie?"

"Apple would be fine," Dixie said, licking her lips. "We've been eating jerky, beans, and boiled potatoes for so long that even a rhubarb pie would be tasty."

"Instead of buying steak, you could try catching trout in the river."

"Yeah," Dixie said, "I could. But I hate to fish. So buy a few pounds of steak and a pie that we can enjoy and whatever is left over we can pack to keep us from starving tomorrow."

"I'll do it," Ruff promised.

He glanced off toward Rio Paso, feeling a little uneasy about leaving his sister alone, even for the short time it would take to buy food and report the shootings to the local authorities. "Dixie, if there's any trouble, I'll be within hearing distance of your rifle shot."

"Just be sure and tell that marshal that those four men charged right through us and pulled their guns first."

"I'll do that."

Ruff touched his heels to High Fire's flanks and galloped off toward Rio Paso, which was situated up from the river, against the pines. When he entered its main street, his handsome Thoroughbred attracted a lot of attention. High Fire was so tall and well muscled that he always drew a crowd of admirers, and today was no exception. Ruff hailed a pedestrian as he rode in, calling, "Where can I find the marshal?"

"Half block up the street on your right," the man said, coming up to lay his hand on the stallion's shoulder. "Quite a horse you have here!"

"Thanks."

"You have a Southern drawl. Is that where you are from?"

"Yes, I'm from Tennessee."

"That a fact?"

"It is," Ruff said proudly. "My sister and I came west in order to keep the last of these horses from being slaughtered on the battlefields."

"It was a terrible war."

"It was," Ruff agreed.

The man offered Ruff a cigar, which he declined. Ruff judged the fellow to be a successful merchant because he wore a bowler, round-toed shoes, and a starched collar.

The man said, "My name is John Delano, and I deal in firearms and also have a small freighting business."

"Pleased to meet you," Ruff said, introducing himself to the man.

"Tell me, Ruff, did you fight for the Confederacy?"

"Being the youngest son, my father tried to keep me from joining the army, but I did see action at Missionary Ridge."

"And your brothers?"

"Three of them killed in battle," Ruff said quietly. "One at Shilo, another at Bull Run, and the last near Lookout Mountain. I got another brother named Houston was captured and thrown into a northern prison. I half expect he's also dead because he was a Confederate spy and they generally shoot spies."

"Yes," Delano said. "I'm afraid they did."

There was a moment of awkward silence, then the man said, "Out in this country, we didn't think too much about the Civil War. We just read about it once a week in the Santa Fe paper."

"Then consider yourself lucky," Ruff told the man. "The Civil War cost my family everything. It drove us out of the South with just a few of the Thoroughbred horses that it took my father a lifetime to breed."

Delano studied Ruff closely, as if trying to make up his mind about something. "You haven't heard the news yet, have you?"

"What news?"

"You can go home to Tennessee now."

"What do you mean?"

"Word reached us yesterday that General Robert E. Lee was forced to surrender his Confederate Army to General Ulysses S. Grant. They signed a peace treaty at a place called Appomattox, Virginia."

Ruff leaned forward on his saddle horn, feeling as if he'd been struck between the eyes. "Are you sure?"

"Of course. You can go home now. That accursed war is definitely over. That's all this town has been talking about since we got the news."

The man said something else, but Ruff didn't hear him. All he could think of was that the war was finally over. So much death and destruction. So many lives wasted—and for what? The Confederacy was no more.

Ruff was so dumbstruck that he forgot about the sheriff and about buying steaks and peaches. He was in a daze as he rode High Fire back to Dixie and their new camp.

When she saw her brother, Dixie dropped the armful of wood she had gathered and rushed over to his side. Ruff looked as if he had aged ten years, and his face was pale, his eyes vacant.

"What's wrong!"

"We lost the war," Ruff mumbled, climbing down from his horse. "We lost."

Dixie buried her face in Ruff's chest and began to cry. And holding her, Ruff cried, too, because he could not help himself. In his mind, he pictured the terrible battles that had killed so many soldiers on both sides of the line. And even those who had been lucky enough to survive had often been sent home physically and mentally broken.

Ruff held Dixie for a good long while. High Man drifted off, and finally, Ruff took a ragged breath and eased Dixie out to arm's length. "I guess this changes everything."

"Yes," Dixie said. "We promised Father that we'd come west and find a place to raise his horses and then supply the Confederate officers and couriers with a superior line of Southern-bred horses. But now, there's no point."

"Except that we still have to carry on the breed."

"Yes," Dixie said, sniffling, "we have to do that."

"But not necessarily out here," Ruff blurted. "I've read a few of the speeches given by President Abraham Lincoln. He sounds like he is a good man, one that would try to heal the wounds of war rather than punish the South. Dixie, if you want, we could finally go back to Tennessee."

"We could." Dixie wiped her eyes. "But do you realize what would happen if we did go home?"

"What do you mean?"

"I mean, what is there to go back to? I'm sure that the Union armies have destroyed our home. It'll be a pile of ashes, as will our barns and fences. There will be nothing left."

"Except the land," Ruff argued. "No army can destroy the land. It'll always come back."

Dixie touched her brother's face and then his ear, which was missing the lobe, shot off during a terrible battle that he had barely survived. "Ruff," she said softly, "you are right about the land, it does come back. But I'm not sure that I want it back."

"I don't understand."

"I mean that it doesn't take a lot of imagination to figure out what will happen to the South now that it is defeated and occupied by the Northerners. Even if Abraham Lincoln really does want to heal the wounds, there are thousand in the North who have lost sons, brothers, and husbands. They'll flood across the South to loot everything of value. There are hatreds so deep on both sides of the Mason-Dixon line that they will never die."

Dixie's expression grew bleak as she continued, "The Northerners will impose their wills on us and grind our rebel noses in the dirt. They'll appoint themselves as our officials and make us grovel. And many of them will take our best land and property."

"If the Northerners tried to grab our land, I'd kill them," Ruff vowed.

"Then others would finally kill you," Dixie said. "You have to understand that they are the victors. And just as sure as night follows day, they'll collect the spoils of war."

"Damn," Ruff said with anguish as the truth of his sister's words sank home. "Damn!"

Dixie waited a moment, then added, "And Ruff, we can't forget the way we left Tennessee."

"You mean about us shooting Captain Denton and those other Confederate soldiers?"

"Yes."

"But there was no choice!"

Dixie nodded in agreement. "Our father had no choice but to try and protect the last of his horses from being taken and lost on the battlefields. So we stood up as a family and we fought our own soldiers."

"Captain Denton ordered his men to open fire on us!"

"Of course he did. And later, when you had to kill Lieutenant Pike and those other Confederate deserters at Aunt

Maybelle's down in Mississippi, that was self-defense, too! But we can't clear our name in either case. And think back. Do you remember what Pike said after you shot him and he lay dying in Aunt Maybelle's yard?"

"How could I ever forget?" Ruff asked, still haunted by the memory. "Pike said that the name Ballou would become a curse word in the South."

"That's right. So we can't ever return to Tennessee. If we weren't shot by the carpetbaggers, then some fool who believed us traitors to the South would ambush us for certain." Dixie took a deep, shuddering breath. "Ruff, to return to Tennessee would be to die."

Ruff twisted away, hands clenched, stomach churning. He went to the river, and although it was cold and swift, he removed his shirt and boots, then plunged into the Rio Grande. An icy fist grabbed and squeezed his heart, and the current spun him around and then sucked him under. Ruff allowed the Rio Grande to pull him straight to its bottom. After a moment, he kicked off the rocky river floor and fought his way back to the surface with fire searing his tortured lungs.

When his head cleared the surface, Ruff expelled a deep breath and glanced back upriver. The Rio Grande roared in his ears, drowning out Dixie's cries, but he knew that she was terrified that he would drown. Ruff almost wanted to drown. The idea that he could never return to his beloved Tennessee was a dagger to his heart. The South needed his help in this time of her great darkness, and Ruff knew that he did not dare to answer her plea.

It also seemed almost inconceivable that the Confederacy had ceased to exist. And yet how could it have been otherwise? The South had been far too agrarian to defeat the highly industrialized North. Its population was less than half that of the North. The Union had more of everything, from railroads and track, to guns, artillery, and gold. Only a gritty Southern determination not to be defeated had enabled the lopsided conflict to run its bloody four years.

"Ruff!" Dixie called. "Please come back! I need you! Our horses need you!"

She was right, Ruff thought, beginning to swim powerfully back toward the shore—they did need him.

When Ruff finally reached the shore, he was physically and mentally spent. He allowed Dixie to scold him and then wrap him in a blanket and lead him back to their camp.

"You're crazy!" she stormed. "You had me scared to death! What do you think would happen to me and our horses if you left us alone out here!"

"I'm sorry," he muttered, pulling the blanket tighter around himself as she built them a fire. "And I even forgot to get those steaks for dinner."

"Then I'll go get them while you pull yourself back together."

"Dixie, I just can't accept the idea that we can never go home."

Dixie's anger passed as quickly as a summer squall. "We just have to make a new home out here in the West. That's what our father wanted us to do."

"I know, but I feel like we're deserting the South at a time that she needs us the most."

"We have to survive," Dixie said. "And we can't do that in Tennessee. Not anymore, we can't. Besides, you're the last man of the family."

"Maybe," Ruff said, "but we still don't know for sure what happened to Houston."

"No," Dixie agreed, "we don't. But after more than a year with no word, we have to accept the idea that he may be dead. Ruff, if it matters any, you were always my favorite brother."

Her words cheered Ruff immensely. He tried not to think any more about that devastating news of the fall of the South. Instead, Ruff told himself that there had been enough killing and that President Lincoln really was a man who fully intended to show compassion to the devastated South, which had already suffered beyond measure.

"The war is finally over," he said, coming to his feet as Dixie saddled High Man. "And Dixie?"

She climbed into the saddle, a tall, dark-complected girl with strong Cherokee features. "Yes?"

"Buy us some whiskey."

"It won't help."

"Maybe not," he said, "but I think the South deserves whatever wake we can give her tonight, don't you?"

"Yes," Dixie said, "I suppose she does."

After Dixie rode away, Ruff busied himself by collecting firewood. Later, he stared into his camp fire, unable to push the war and the defeat of the Confederacy from his troubled thoughts. He recalled how, at its beginning, both the North and the South had believed it would be a short conflict. All of Dixie celebrated with their decisive victory at Fort Sumter, a small federal army fort on an island in the harbor of Charleston. Shortly after that, the Confederates had also been victorious at Bull Run Creek, driving shattered Union forces back to Washington. Oh, but those early and almost surprisingly easy victories had been heady for the South!

Soon, however, the North's superior size and strength began to turn the tide back to her favor. Battle after battle had been waged and the larger, better trained and provisioned Union armies started to invade and conquer the South. Finally, by 1863, General Grant had captured the Mississippi town of Vicksburg, and that great river belonged to the Union, blockading a vital avenue of Southern commerce. Along the eastern seaboard, the United States Navy closed Southern harbors creating hunger and then famine. The Confederate Army was reduced to near starvation. By then it was obvious that the North would eventually prevail, but this realization had only stiffened the Confederacy's resolve to fight on to glory.

Now, what price glory? A quarter million Confederate soldiers buried but never to be forgotten. At least as many Yankee soldiers also dead. And all for . . . what?

Ruff stared into the flames as dusk fell across the high mountains of New Mexico. A coyote sounded its mournful cry, and that caused Ruff to lift his eyes to the rugged line of silhouetted peaks that ringed this immense New Mexico Valley. While it was true that men died by the gun just as surely as they did in a war, at least in places like this Ruff felt no ghosts from the past. There was only good land, sweet grass, and plenty of water and timber.

Ruff took a deep breath and smelled the pines. Somehow, some way, he had to go on with his life and put Tennessee out of his mind forever.

THREE

They ate a quiet dinner that night because both Ruff and Dixie were absorbed by their troubled thoughts about the end of the Civil War and what their future might be in the West.

"I remember the summer when I was five years old," Ruff reminisced. "Houston and I used to go down to the pond and catch frogs. We'd start out rolling our pant legs up to our knees and wading in the water, but before we knew it, we'd be up to our necks."

"Father always said we were never to go swimming in that pond," Dixie said. "He said there were water moccasins hiding in the tules and under the lily pads."

"There were." Ruff pitched wood onto the dying fire. "It was near the end of that summer that I almost got bit by one."

"You did?"

"Yep. One minute I was swimming and the next it was coming at me, faster than anything. I'd never even seen one of the things before, but I knew it was a snake and that it was going to bite me."

"Did it?"

"No," Ruff said quietly. "Houston grabbed up a stout branch and jumped into the pond. He landed right on top of me. I lost consciousness and went under. Next thing I knew, Houston was pounding on my back. I coughed up water, and when I could stand, Houston told me that my right shoulder was sitting about two inches higher than my

21

left. That's when I realized that it was broken. Houston felt real bad about that, but I told him not to worry because I wouldn't tell Father how he landed on me."

"What about the water moccasin?"

"He said he hit it with that branch and the snake disappeared. We both decided that he killed the water moccasin."

"That was pretty brave of Houston."

"He's not afraid of anything," Ruff said. "Near the end of the war, when we rode off with Mason to get back our Thoroughbreds, Houston led us into a Union Army camp, bold as brass. He bluffed a pair of sentries into giving us back our horses, saying we had orders to breed them in the moonlight."

"Breed them in the moonlight?"

Ruff chuckled. "Houston knew he was talking to a couple of city boys. They didn't know that a stallion doesn't care if it's night or day when it comes time to breed. I almost laughed and gave us both away."

"And got yourself shot."

"That's right." Ruff was silent a moment, glad to remember that one funny moment of the war. "Houston had a way with words. He could spin a windy like no one I've ever heard before, or since."

"He also had a way with cards and pretty women."

"Yeah."

"Did you ever see another water moccasin in our pond?"

"No. I stayed away from the pond for the next few years. It seemed like a bad place to hunt frogs from then on."

"I feel that way about Tennessee," Dixie confessed. "Not a night goes by that when I close my eyes to sleep I don't see father being shot down in our yard, when the soldiers tried to take the last of our horses."

Ruff didn't know what to say.

"But I also have good dreams of home," Dixie said quickly. "One night I heard the voice of our Cherokee mother singing on the wind."

"I remember her voice, too." Ruff sighed. "And sometimes I dream about cool mornings and our Thoroughbreds galloping around our track. I can hear our father yelling instructions as I exercised the horses."

"Thoroughbreds were his life."

"They were," Ruff agreed. "They and us kids were all that he lived for after Mother died."

"And I think he preferred the horses over us kids," Dixie said with a fond smile.

"After he lost Mother, then Mica and then John, I think Justin decided that the war might kill off the rest of us boys. That's why he was so determined that Houston and I stay at Wildwood Farm and not join up to fight."

Dixie gazed up at the stars. "If father were here with us in New Mexico, he wouldn't go back to the South. I think he'd find a place and build a ranch. He'd make a mark no matter where he settled."

"And you think we should do the same." It wasn't a question because Ruff knew what his sister meant.

"Yes, I do. You see, it's the person, not the setting or the circumstances, that counts," Dixie decided out loud. "Strong people succeed wherever they must. Weak people, or those that are broken by the world, fail."

"We're strong people."

"Yes," Dixie said, "we are."

Ruff lay back on his bedroll and also turned his eyes to the starry heavens. "After Mica died, I remember Emma telling me that every time we lost someone we really, really loved, they turned into a bright star."

Emma had been their house servant and had taken the place of their mother after her death. The old woman had been wise, but she had also been superstitious and believed in spooks, goblins, and witches. "She really said that?"

"Yes and about John and our mother. She said that all good people turned into stars."

"What about bad ones?"

Ruff couldn't suppress a grin. "Emma said the bad people turn into dirty old stones."

"Ha! So what did you say about such nonsense?"

"I called it all a fairy tale."

"Did Emma get mad?"

"Nope. She just raised her eyebrows and said that unless I had actually counted all the stars so that I knew there wasn't another one that was Mica, then she guessed that I had no business calling it a fairy tale."

"No one can count all the stars."

"Emma knew that."

"Huh," Dixie grunted. "I like that."

She raised her forefinger up to the sky. "If I believed Emma, then every night I could almost touch Father and Mother, Mica and John. One by one, I could touch them good night."

Ruff smiled to himself and went to sleep, his mind a collage of fragmented childhood memories. He knew that the end of the Civil War was going to affect him in ways that he did not yet fully understand. Maybe, if Houston had been a prisoner of war this past year, he would be released and come west looking to find them. They had been sending regular letters to Aunt Maybelle's Mississippi plantation, and she had orders to give them to Houston, telling him to follow them into New Mexico. Also, their Thoroughbreds were uncommon and not soon forgotten.

Ruff suspected that a lot of young Southern boys would be leaving the wreckage of a vanquished South. They'd come looking for a fresh start, hoping to put their own tragic pasts far, far behind.

"Ruff?"

"Yeah?"

"I think that Houston must have jammed that awful water moccasin so deep into the mud that it drowned. I never saw even one swimming in that pond in all the many years that I can remember."

"That's because you never went frogging."

There was a long silence and then Dixie said, "That's true. Good night."

Ruff awoke to the sound of a six-gun cocking beside his ear, and then he heard a gravelly voice. "Don't even think of moving, young fella, or I'll blow your brains out."

Ruff's eyes popped open, and he stared up at a big, heavyset man with a thick silver beard and squinting brown eyes. Ruff did not fail to note that the barrel of the man's gun was rock-steady.

"Who are you, stranger?"

"Rufus Ballou." Ruff attempted a weak smile that failed. "And who might you be?"

"I'll ask the damned questions. Who's the girl?"

"My sister, Dixie."

"Where you from?"

"Tennessee."

"And you got here by way of?"

"We are following the Rio Grande and heading up toward Colorado. We're looking for a place to build a Thoroughbred horse ranch."

"You got money?" So, Ruff thought, we are dealing with a common thief.

"Some, but not much."

"Then how do you figure to buy land?"

"Can I sit up and start a fire?" Ruff asked, noting that sunrise was barely under way. "I'll boil some coffee."

"Shut up and roll over on your belly."

"What for?"

"I'm the marshal of Rio Paso and you're under arrest. Put your hands behind your back so I can handcuff you."

"But . . ."

"One more word and I'll use the barrel of my six-gun to put a furrow across your forehead deep enough to plant corn seed."

Ruff knew that the lawman wasn't bluffing, so he rolled over and kept his mouth shut. The marshal put the handcuffs on real tight, and Ruff knew it would be useless to shout a warning to Dixie. This marshal was a hard man, and he might even open fire with that Colt pistol.

"Miss Ballou, wake up!" the marshal ordered, gently nudging Dixie with the toe of his boot.

Dixie was awake. She must have heard conversation because she had collected her gun and slipped it under her bedroll. And now, as the marshal stood over her, he gaped to see a loaded six-gun pointing up at his big belly. The marshal hadn't expected trouble and had holstered his gun after handcuffing Ruff, so now he was caught flat-footed.

"Don't you move, Marshal," Dixie warned, coming to her feet and holding the gun steady. "Let's see your badge."

"How can I show it to you if I'm not supposed to move?"

"All right. Left hand, slow and easy. Just remember this: You're a big target and I'm a good shot."

"Damned if I don't believe you," the marshal grunted, pulling back his coat to reveal a silver star. "Now, Missy, are you satisfied?"

"Nope," Dixie said. "And I won't be until you reach across that big gut of yours and slowly remove your gun."

The marshal bristled. "You're getting yourself into a bad fix, young lady."

"Maybe," Dixie said, throwing a glance at Ruff. "But you didn't need to handcuff my brother."

"I should have handcuffed you instead," the marshal spat. "Now what are you going to do?"

"First, I'm going to take your keys and get those handcuffs off Ruff. Then after that, it's sort of up to you."

Ruff climbed to his feet with a grin. He walked over to Dixie saying, "The key is probably in his vest pocket."

It was. Dixie had the handcuffs unlocked in a few moments, and she was very pleased with herself. The marshal was another matter entirely. He looked madder than a teased badger and just about as feisty.

"You two are sure digging yourselves deeper into trouble."

Ruff took the marshal's gun and said, "It seems to me that this whole part of New Mexico is big trouble. Four men jumped us yesterday, and they were sure trouble."

"You killed three of them," the marshal said accusingly. "I found their bodies last night and then followed your tracks to this camp."

"Those men attacked us," Dixie interrupted. "If you could read instead of just follow tracks, you would have been able to figure that much out."

"Mind your tongue, young woman! I'm an old man and the law in these parts, and I will not brook any sassin'."

"You'll brook whatever we dish out," Dixie said. "If you had any sense, you'd have just let my brother explain how things were and let it go at that. Do we look like outlaws?"

The marshal scowled. "I seen peach-faced kids not much older than you, Missy, that killed men for fun."

"Well, we're not that kind! And as far as we're concerned, we can't get out of New Mexico fast enough."

"You get any of that bank money?"

"They robbed your bank?"

"Robbed both of our banks," the marshal corrected. "Luckily, there wasn't a fortune in either one of them. Most folks in Rio Paso do their main banking in Taos and just keep their small money here because our banks ain't worth spit. The outlaws got a few thousand dollars, but they gunned down both our bankers. It was just a hell of a cold-blooded deal."

"I'm real sorry to hear that," Ruff said. "I'm also sorry to disappoint you, but we didn't get back any of the stolen money. I expect that the lone man that escaped took it all. Too bad you didn't follow his tracks instead of ours."

"Yeah," the marshal said, unable to keep the bitterness out of his voice, "I can see that you and your sassy sister are all choked up over it."

Ruff bristled. "We are sorry, but we sure helped even the score. So what happens now?"

"Your sister puts that gun away and we ride back to my town and have a long talk."

"No more handcuffs?" Dixie asked.

"No."

"All right then," Dixie said, holstering her gun, "but we'll be hanging onto your pistol until we are sure that you have seen the error of your ways."

"Dammit!" the marshal stormed. "I'm not about to ride back into my own town unarmed. I'm the law in Rio Paso."

Ruff could see that there was the potential for embarrassment, so he handed the marshal back his weapon. "I'll get the horses saddled," he said, "and when we get to town, you can buy the coffee, Marshal."

"Fair enough. By the way, my full name is Joad. Marshal Augustus Joad. Everyone in this part of the country calls me Marshal Gus."

"Well, Marshal Gus," Ruff said, "we really are sorry about those dead bankers."

"Fair enough, but why didn't you ride into town and report you killed three of the four bank robbers?"

"We worried that you might jump to the conclusion that we were somehow to blame."

"Blame hell! If you'd have come into town with that bank money, you'd have been popular enough to have been elected the town mayor!"

Ruff looked to his sister. "We'll try to help you all that we can, Marshal Gus."

"Fair enough," the lawman said as he turned and walked heavily back to his horse, his big roweled spurs making scratches across the bare earth.

FOUR

It took Ruff and Dixie only a few minutes to break camp and saddle the stallions.

"Them sure are fine-looking horses," Marshal Gus said. "I'm riding a runty buckskin, and I'd admire to own a tall horse, if he could stand up to this hard country."

"They'll stand up just fine," Ruff said confidently.

"How much are them stallions worth?"

"I wouldn't put a price on either of them."

"Then what about the mares? I sort of favor sorrels, and you've got three or four damned good-looking ones."

"They'll cost you a thousand dollars," Dixie said.

"A thousand dollars!" Gus barked a laugh. "Jeezus, girl! I can buy good horses all day long in this country for fifty dollars."

"I suspect you can," Dixie said, not backing up an inch on her price. "But these mares will foal the best running horses you ever did see. If you breed them to a good sire, you'll never have to work again."

"Pretty big talk, young lady."

"It's true," Dixie argued. "Why, on a Ballou Thoroughbred, you'd be able to run down and arrest every outlaw that committed a crime in Rio Paso."

"If I paid you a thousand dollars," Gus said, "then I'd have to take flight 'cause the only way I could get my hands on that much money would be to steal it. Those mares are handsome, but they don't lay golden eggs, and that's what they'd have to do to be worth a thousand dollars."

Ruff couldn't help but chuckle. "Marshal," he said, "these are Thoroughbred racehorses. And I know that you folks in New Mexico enjoy the great tradition of horse racing."

"Well, that's a fact," the marshal agreed. "But it'd take a while to win that much money."

"Nothing good ever comes quick," Dixie said. "Now, if you'll excuse me, I'll get the mares rounded up so we can get to town and finish our business before riding on to Colorado."

The marshal watched as Dixie quickly made the gather. "Your sister is a pretty good hand."

"She can ride some."

"I can see that. Does she race these stallions?"

"Yes. But why do you ask?"

"I suspect they race like gentlemen back east," the marshal said, "but we're a lot rougher on these western tracks."

"Thanks for the warning," Ruff said.

When the mares were rounded up and everything was ready, the marshal led off toward nearby Rio Paso. As they approached, a sizable crowd came out to meet them.

"Kind of early in the morning for this many people to be up, isn't it?" Ruff asked.

"Yep. Normally the streets are damn near empty before eight o'clock. But the bank robberies and killings have everyone stirred up. I expect that these folks are wondering if you are involved."

"Make sure to tell them all that we are not," Dixie said, watching the grim-faced and excited crowd that was starting to ask their marshal questions all at the same time.

"Calm down!" the marshal yelled. "I can't understand when you're all talkin' at once."

He gestured toward a man in a nice suit with chin whiskers and a protruding Adam's apple. "Mayor Morton, what's everyone so excited about?"

Morton was a tall, gawky fellow in his late forties. "The banker, Mr. Rudd—he's alive!"

"Alive? How the hell can that be?"

Morton said in a tone that reflected his own amazement, "The doc worked a miracle. The bullet that hit him in the chest plowed through an Ingersol pocket watch that was in his shirt pocket. There was blood, but that watch slowed the bullet down. Anyway, Mr. Rudd is offering a two thousand dollar reward for the return of his depositors' money."

"That's damned generous! But what about them three fellas I deputized? Didn't they overtake that last robber?"

"Nope."

"Maybe they did and they're just trying to hang onto the money for themselves," Gus mused out loud.

"I'm just sure that's not true," the mayor replied. "They said they rode for more'n a hundred miles trying to cross that last fella's trail, but it disappeared somewhere up near Antelope Peak. One of them lost a horse over the side of a cliff, another took sick with a fever. That last deputy you sent just rode on to Taos, saying he could get a better job anyways."

"Blast!" the marshal swore. "The fella with all the money is probably clear off to hell and gone by now, and we'll never find him."

"We still might," Morton said. "You see, there's a bunch of the local boys lit out after that reward money. Charlie Benson is leading them."

"Charlie?" The marshal stared, and when Morton nodded, Gus snorted with derision. "Why, Charlie Benson couldn't find his way out of a shitter!"

Morton shrugged his narrow shoulders. "That'd be about

right, Gus. But he and some boys took off after that last fella, and there was blood in their eyes. They intend to collect that reward, and they might get lucky."

"And the sky might fall," Gus snapped.

Morton looked to Dixie and then to Ruff. "Who are these two?"

The marshal jerked a thumb in Ruff's direction. "This is Ruff Ballou. He's the one that killed them other three bank robbers. Just his luck that the one carrying the loot was the only one that escaped."

Morton and the others nodded, and someone said, "You almost earned two thousand dollars, young fella. Too bad."

Dixie's anger flashed. "You ought to pay a reward for the men that killed the bankers. And that being the case, we killed three of the four. That means we ought to get fifteen hundred dollars."

"I ain't the one that set the terms, miss. You want something for killing them bank robbers, you can take your case to Mr. Rudd, but it won't do no good."

"That isn't fair!"

A young, well-dressed man stepped forward with a gleaming smile. "Miss, did I understand you to say that you killed one of the bank robbers?"

"Yes, with this saddle carbine."

A murmur of surprise and then appreciation passed through the crowd. The well-dressed man thumbed his Stetson back, revealing a mass of curly black hair. "I admire a woman who can stand up and protect herself."

"Thank you."

"And I'd be pleased to call on you while you're in these parts, miss. My name is Bob Justin. I own a ranch over near Three Forks."

Ruff took an instant dislike to the man who was shining

she isn't interested in you or your ranch, we're leaving for Colorado."

sense in doing that," Bob said, never taking off Dixie. "Why, there's nothing in Colorado that will compare to this upper Rio Grande Valley. You ought to stay and enjoy the scenery, miss."

Dixie blushed. "It is pretty country. My brother and I were just saying we'd like to buy a horse ranch and this wouldn't be a bad place."

"You're right."

"No we weren't," Ruff objected. "We've definitely decided on Denver."

Justin was ignoring Ruff. "Miss, I'd be happy to show you a couple of pieces of flat land over near our spread."

"I said we aren't staying."

The cattleman ignored Ruff and tipped his hat far forward. "If you change your mind about leaving, my offer stands, Miss Ballou."

Ruff would have taken Justin down a peg except that he wanted to finish this trouble and ride north. "Marshal, could we get down to business so that Dixie and I can be on our way?"

"Sorry," Gus apologized. "Let's go to my office. Won't take but a few minutes to hear everything."

High Man and High Fire were nervous and so were the mares, because of the large and agitated crowd. Several times, Ruff had to warn people to step back or they might get kicked.

Spotting an empty corral, Ruff said, "Marshal Gus? Can I turn our mares loose in that corral?"

"Sure," Gus said. "Will your stallions raise hell if we leave them tied to that hitchrail?"

"They'll be fine so long as people don't pester 'em."

It only took a few minutes to corral the mares and then tie their matched sorrel stallions in front of the marshal's office. All the while, people kept asking Ruff and Dixie questions about the dead bank robbers they'd shot. It didn't help that Bob Justin attached himself to Dixie like a leech.

"Come on," Ruff ordered. "Let's go inside and get this over with so we can ride on."

"Well, wait a minute," Dixie protested. "Bob thinks that he'd like to buy one of our mares."

Ruff looked at the handsome young rancher. "Do you really have a thousand dollars cash?"

"Damn right. And I may even go after the reward offered by Mr. Rudd," Justin said, winking at Dixie. "It would probably buy a couple of your mares, huh, Miss Ballou?"

"Nope," Dixie said. "Our mares are worth every penny of a thousand dollars. They're related to the stallions we're riding. And neither High Man nor his son High Fire have ever been beat at over half a mile."

Justin raised his eyebrows. "That's big talk. Who have they raced?"

"A lot of horses you've never heard of in New Mexico," Ruff said bluntly.

"Well then, no offense to you or your horses, but in New Mexico, you have to prove your brag. You see, we have some very fast horses that sell for a whole lot less money than you're asking."

Ordinarily, Ruff would have jumped at this challenge and arranged a race for High Fire. But not today. He did not like Justin, and he most certainly did not want the arrogant young rancher to own one of their mares, at any price.

"Our mares are not for sale," he decided out loud. "As soon as we've helped your marshal, we're heading for Colorado."

Justin glanced at Dixie, and when she said nothing, he drawled, "Damn shame you're in such a hurry to leave Rio Paso. The locals would pay big money to see your horses race against the best in the Rio Grande Valley."

"Maybe another time."

"I just happen to have a pretty fast horse of my own."

"Not interested," Ruff said. He looked to the marshal and said, "Anytime you're ready."

"Are you afraid of racing my horse?" Justin asked with a mocking grin.

Ruff could feel himself tensing with anger, and it must have showed, because the marshal pushed between them and said, "Bob, let things be. These people aren't interested in a horse race and the timing is dead wrong."

"Why?"

"Because we've just lost a banker, and a lot of upset people have just lost their deposits! You ought to be able to figure that much out for yourself, for crying out loud."

The rancher's cheeks colored. "Marshal, I don't much appreciate being talked to thataway."

"Well," Gus said, "these are my witnesses and I need to talk to them. Afterward, you can flirt with Miss Dixie all you want, unless her brother takes a different view."

"As a matter of fact," Ruff said, "I do. My sister and I have been thrust into something here not of our choosing. As soon as our business is finished, we'll be riding north."

"Fine with me," Gus grunted. "Mayor?"

"Yes?"

"You probably ought to hear what the Ballous have to say before they ride on."

"All right," Morton agreed, not sounding very enthused at the idea. "Whatever you say."

The marshal waved everyone inside, but when Justin tried to join them, Gus said, "Bob, wait outside with everyone else."

The young cattleman stiffened as if slapped in the face. "Listen, Marshal, I lost as much money yesterday as anyone in that bank robbery. I need to decide whether or not to go after that last outlaw."

"After we're finished and these folks ride on, I'll tell you everything I learn. Is that fair?"

Justin wasn't pleased, but he could hardly protest that he was being unfairly treated. So, with a curt nod of his head, he tramped on outside.

"Bob is a little forward," Gus explained. "Miss Dixie, I hope you didn't take offense by him."

"No, he was cute."

Ruff clenched his jaw and bit into a hard silence. He didn't like hearing that kind of talk from his kid sister. As far as Ruff was concerned, Dixie was just a girl in britches and pigtails. She'd grow up someday and become a woman, but there was no need to hurry the process.

"Now," Gus said, easing into his chair and kicking his feet up on his desk as they all took up chairs, "there will be a pot of coffee comin' along momentarily from old Wong Woo. Wong owns the cafe up the street. He might even bring along some cookies, 'cause he knows I left this morning hours before breakfast and I'll be as starved as a big wolf in a bad winter."

Marshal Gus scratched his protruding belly and sighed. "All right, Mr. Ballou, for Mayor Morton's benefit, why don't you go over what happened again, from the very beginning."

Ruff nodded and carefully related how the four bank robbers had charged them and then how he'd chased one and knocked him off his horse. "It was an accident that he broke his neck. It wasn't my intention to kill anyone until they pulled guns."

"Did you see anything else that might prove useful?"

"Nope. But one man did speak a woman's name as he was dying."

Both the marshal and the mayor leaned forward. Gus said, "And that was?"

"Jessica. He said, 'Tell Jessica that I . . . ,' and then he died."

"That's all?" Gus asked, looking disappointed. "No last name or where she could be found or anything?"

"Nope," Ruff said. "He said exactly what I just said. Nothing more and nothing less."

Ruff waited a moment, and when the silence deepened, he added, "I take it that there isn't a Jessica in this town?"

"That's right," the marshal said. "Not a single damned one. He was probably talking about a dance hall girl down in Santa Fe or Albuquerque."

Morton said, "Sounds to me like you kids were just unlucky to be in the wrong place at the wrong time. And lucky enough to be able to defend yourselves."

"I don't think," the marshal said, "that luck had much to do with it. My guess is that, while this pair may look as innocent as church mice, they're foolers. You don't take on three hardcases like they did and come out without a scratch."

"We're nothing special, but our father did teach us how to handle firearms," Ruff explained. "Those men should have just kept riding, but they doubled back, and we drilled two of them because they were trying to fire from atop running horses, while we were dismounted and were able to take a steady aim. It really wasn't much of a contest."

Morton and Gus exchanged glances, and then the marshal said, "Your sister gave me the impression that you can track. Is that right?"

Ruff nodded.

"Maybe you'd like to go after that big reward."

"I'm no bounty hunter."

"I see." The marshal started to say something else, but a shout brought him out of his chair. The door burst open, and a breathless man said, "Marshal, there's something comin' that you and the mayor better take a look at."

Gus glanced at Morton and said, "Sounds like bad news."

When they all went outside, they saw two men slumped over in their saddles leading four horses carrying dead men.

"That's the bunch that Charlie led out of here!" the mayor exclaimed.

"Damn!" Gus swore. "And neither one of them riders is Charlie, so my guess is he's been killed. We have a real mess on our hands now, Mayor."

"What could have happened?" the mayor breathed, looking faint.

"I expect that Charlie and his friends were lured into an ambush," the marshal said as he joined the crowd that was hurrying toward the approaching horsemen.

Dixie frowned. "Ruff, how could one bank robber shoot up all those men?"

"My guess is that the lone bank robber caught up with some friends and they helped him set the ambush."

"I want to leave Rio Paso and put this bloodshed behind," Dixie said.

Ruff's instinctive reaction surprised even himself. "If you don't mind, let's wait a few more minutes. I'd like to find out what actually happened."

"Why?" Dixie asked with exasperation.

"Because, like it or not, we're a part of this, and I'm too curious a man not to want to hear out the story."

"Dammit!" Dixie swore. "Curiosity killed the cat."

"Yeah, but I don't even like cats," Ruff said as he hurried up the street to do whatever he could to help the two wounded riders.

FIVE

"Stand back!" the marshal bellowed, knocking men aside as he hurried toward the riders. "Goddammit, someone send for the doctor!"

"And the mortician," another man yelled. "He's the one that's gonna have the most work."

Ruff joined in to help the two badly wounded men from their saddles. One of them was obviously dying, for he had been shot three times, the most serious shot being through the stomach. He was ghost-white and shaking like he had the ague. Semi-delirious, the man kept mumbling, "No chance. No chance."

"Where and how many?" the marshal asked in a surprisingly gentle voice after the dying young man was carried over to the boardwalk and eased down in the shade.

"Six, maybe seven. No chance."

Gus laid his big hand on the dying man's shoulder. "Walt, we're going to get 'em. One way or the other, I'll either shoot 'em, or bring 'em back to hang."

But Walt was past caring. He was in agony, and it wasn't until someone pressed a bottle of whiskey to his lips and he had a few gulps that he even became aware of his surroundings. He rolled his head from side to side, looking at the curious ring of faces. "Hi, boys, guess I'm a goner, huh?"

Walt tried to laugh but coughed blood. Nobody else laughed either, and some men turned and walked quickly away.

"Marshal Gus?"

"Yeah?"

"Charlie was a . . . a goddamn fool!" the dying man choked. "He lead us right into a box canyon. They . . . they was . . . waitin'! Like shootin' fish in . . ."

"A barrel," Gus finished as the man died with a shudder.

The second man wasn't in much better shape, and when the doctor arrived, he examined him and then shook his head. "Jeremiah, you got any family we don't know about?"

Jeremiah had taken a bullet in the shoulder and another in the back. He shook his head. "We was drunk," he whispered, tears streaking down his tanned cheeks. "Drunk and hollerin' and such. Our own damn faults!"

"Yeah," the marshal said, "and I'll bet that Charlie Benson was the drunkest and loudest."

Jeremiah's lips twisted in bitterness. "Charlie Benson was laughin' and swearin' and so damned stinkin' drunk he kept fallin' off'n his horse. The first bullet they fired exploded through the bottle at his mouth and tore his face to ribbons. Second bullet knocked him over the back of his horse, and I think I caught the third bullet."

"Where was this box canyon?"

Jeremiah sniffled and reached up to wipe tears from his eyes. He stared at his wet fingers and said, "Jeezus, Marshal Gus, look at me. I'm cryin' like a little baby! I broke my leg on a horse and rode all day 'afore I could get whiskey, and I didn't cry any then. I thought I was so goddamn tough, Gus, but I ain't, 'cause I'm cryin' like a baby!"

Jeremiah tried to turn his face away, but Gus cradled his face with both hands. "You're still tough, kid. Where is that box canyon?"

"Fifty miles north just above the fork of Little Alder Creek."

"You think it was their hideout?"

Jeremiah started to answer, but he was overcome with a spasm so powerful that it caused his heels to drum the dirt. When the spasm passed, Ruff thought the man was dead, but after a moment, Jeremiah's eyelids fluttered open and he cried, "Git 'em, Gus!"

"I will," the marshal vowed. "It shoulda been me, not Charlie, that was leading you fool boys."

Jeremiah clenched his teeth until the muscles in his cheeks stood out like stretched rawhide. He nodded his head and then he began to cough.

The marshal tore his handkerchief out of his back pocket and shoved it at someone, yelling, "Wet it in the trough and bring it back. Hurry!"

When the man returned with the sopping handkerchief, Gus carefully wiped Jeremiah's tearstained face clean and said, "The hurting is almost over now, son. You're goin' home, and we'll give you a proper resting place."

The kid reached up and grabbed the marshal's shoulder. Ruff saw Jeremiah's fingers bite deep into flesh, but Gus didn't flinch as the young man said, "I just ain't ready to die yet."

"Nobody ever is."

"But I'm only twenty! Gus, I never even fell in love!"

The marshal took a deep, ragged breath. "Love hurts, too. It generally falls short of the promise."

Jeremiah seemed to think about that for a minute as fresh tears welled up in his eyes. "It just hurts like hell, Gus," he whispered. "Onc't, I stepped barefooted on a burnin' ember. It was a fierce pain, but not like this."

Gus gave him whiskey and advice. "Drink, don't talk."

Jeremiah drank, nearly half a bottle, and that seemed to help after a few minutes, because his body relaxed. "Gus,

I want you to have my horse. You're the one that first put me on a horse. Remember?"

"Yeah, snot-nosed kid."

"Yeah." Jeremiah gritted a smile. "And my rifle and pistol. Saddle and . . ."

"Here, drink some more. You always did get too generous when you drank, kid."

"Just use 'em to get them fellas, Gus. That's all I'm askin' in return. You . . . kill them bastards!"

Ruff turned away as Jeremiah's back came completely off the ground and his lips drew back in a death grimace. He'd seen many soldiers die on the battlefields of the South, and he knew that Jeremiah was down to a few precious breaths. His skin color turned grayish, a dullness coated his eyes, and every breath the man took required a tremendous effort of will.

"He's gone," someone whispered.

The people of Rio Paso turned to stare at the marshal, and the old lawman showed how not to roll a cigarette. He spilled tobacco, and the match in his hand danced as Gus lit his smoke. Suddenly aware that everyone was staring at him, he growled, "What the hell is everyone staring at!"

"We gonna bury 'em today?" someone dared to ask.

"Well," Gus snapped, exhaling smoke through both nostrils. "Unless people want to stare at 'em, why the hell not!"

The marshal took another drag, and it seemed to calm his anger. "Listen, when Charlie's pa discovers that his son has been killed, there will be hell to pay. Now, let's get those bodies over to the mortician's office and everyone just . . . just do what you normally do, and we'll have the funeral later."

Ruff looked to Dixie and shrugged his shoulders, then started after the marshal. Dixie followed him, and when they overtook the lawman, she said, "I take it that Mr. Benson is a pretty fierce old man."

"Elias Benson is a heller," Gus replied. "He owns a timber mill and a gold mine. Stingiest and luckiest man I ever did see. He struck gold on his first prospecting trip into these mountains about fifty years ago and made a fortune. Never spent much of it—but his sons sure tried."

"How many children did he have besides Charlie?"

"Two and he's lost 'em both. One went to fight for the Confederacy and was killed at Bull Run; the other was wild as an Apache and got himself knifed to death in a Santa Fe cantina over a Mexican girl. Losin' that young fool Charlie is going to break that old man's heart and make him inhuman."

Ruff glanced at his sister, then back at the marshal. "I sure wish that I'd have killed that last fella. It would have saved a bunch of lives."

"Jeremiah was easily the best of them boys." The marshal cleared his throat. "I've known and liked that kid since he was an orphan boy left by his pa after his ma died."

"I'm sorry."

"Don't be," the marshal said heavily. "You and that sister of yours have already done a hell of a lot more than your share."

"We were just trying to protect ourselves and our horses. Nothing heroic or special about that."

Ruff looked closer at the lawman. Gus's face was pasty, and the man looked either unwell or upset. "Marshal, are you feeling all right?"

"Sure! And maybe you were just protecting yourselves, but you did my job. You see, I was playing hookey during those bank robberies."

"Hookey?"

"Yeah," the marshal said, his voice harsh with self-recrimination. "I hadn't had a day off in weeks, and I just said to hell with it and went fishing upriver. The fish weren't biting, but I had a fine afternoon and was dozin' like an old dog in the sun. The shots woke me, and by the time that I could get back to town, the banks were busted and their managers both shot."

"The robbers must have overheard you say something about going fishing."

The marshal's face hardened. "I'm sure that's the way of it, and I've been blamin' myself ever since. I guess maybe I should have been put out to pasture several years ago. Maybe if I'd been replaced by a young fire-eater like yourself, then none of this would have happened."

Ruff thought that the marshal was being pretty hard on himself. "What about your deputies?"

"I don't have any regular ones. I deputize men when I can, and look what happens to 'em. They get liquored up and ride into traps and get shot all to hell."

"They were grown men," Dixie said, her voice soft but uncompromising. "They should have known that getting liquored up would backfire on a manhunt."

"I expect so," the marshal said, "and I appreciate you trying to make me feel better about this whole mess, but this wouldn't have happened if I was young again. I'd have been on the job and would have killed them four sonsabitches in town or chased 'em down myself."

Ruff heard a shout and turned to see a buckboard, driver, and two horses come flying into view. The driver wasn't sparing the whip, and Ruff could guess who was descending like a summer squall upon an already shaken Rio Paso.

"Elias Benson?" Dixie asked.

"Yep," the marshal replied. "And since you're a young lady, it'd be best if you and your brother left town right now. The old man has a terrible temper. He might even go crazy and start shootin'. I'd be his target, but he's half-blind, and so I would probably be the last one he'd manage to drop."

"There's no reason for him to abuse you, Marshal. You've done your best."

"Which ain't been none too good." Gus looked around to make sure no one was close enough to overhear him. "Why, you two youngsters even got the drop on me this morning."

Ruff didn't know what to say, so he just kept quiet and watched as the buckboard slewed over a low rise, wheels ripping up sod before the wagon came bouncing into town. Everyone cleared the street, and it burned Ruff to see the way that old Benson was mistreating his fine team of horses.

"I understand how upset he must be about losing the last of his boys," Ruff said, "but that's still no reason to punish that team."

"You'd best not advise him of that fact," the marshal said, reaching down and easing his six-gun up a little in his holster. "Elias isn't the kind who takes advice."

Old Elias Benson wasn't an especially big man, but his weather-beaten face was dominated by a hooked beak and eyes so cold, black, and piercing that they reminded Ruff of a hunting hawk. Even before his buckboard stopped, Elias jumped out of it and charged the marshal, hand clawing for the gun on his side.

Marshal Gus wasn't caught by surprise. His own six-gun came up surprisingly quick, and he shoved it out at arm's length, cocked back the hammer, and shouted, "You clear leather, you're as dead as your boy!"

That stopped Elias Benson in his tracks. Ruff heard a strangled sound tear out of the old man's throat and saw spittle spray out of his mouth as he screeched, "Your fault, Augustus! You worthless old son of a bitch, it was your job, not that of them boys!"

"I asked 'em to wait while I followed another trail. All they had to do was wait a few lousy hours and I'd have come back to lead 'em."

But Elias wasn't listening he was so crazed by anger and grief. "Their blood stains your soul, goddamn you!"

"Your boy was dead drunk, Elias. He led the others into a damn trap. Charlie was as much at fault as me."

This was too much for Elias. With an enraged bellow, he grabbed the butt of his six-gun, and Ruff knew that he had to act or someone else was about to die, probably an innocent spectator.

Ruff was standing only about ten feet from Elias, and he threw himself headlong at the man, driving his shoulder into Elias's hip and knocking him down. The old man tried to club Ruff with his pistol. When Ruff grabbed his wrist, Elias hooked a thumb at his eyes, his nail tearing a gash through Ruff's eyebrow.

Ruff kept a hard grip on Elias's wrist so he wouldn't get shot, and then he drew back his fist and smashed the crazy old coot between the eyes. Elias bellowed and tried to choke Ruff. The man was old, but he was incredibly strong, and it took all of Ruff's strength to pin him to the ground and smash him a second time.

"Get off'n me, you bastard!" Elias screamed, trying to buck him off.

Ruff drew back his fist one last time. "Mr. Benson, I'm going to splatter your beak if you don't simmer down!"

"And I'm going to get up and shoot your guts out!"

Ruff would have hit the man except that the marshal dragged him to his feet and, pointing his six-gun down at Elias, said, "You calm down, or I'll put your bacon on ice."

"This ain't over," Elias said, coming to his senses. "I'll get you another time, Gus."

"You can try," the marshal said, "but it'd be your last mistake. Now, get up."

The man climbed to his feet, and he was still mad but clearly woozy from the two punches that Ruff had administered. "Who the hell are you!" he demanded.

"Ruff Ballou. Me and my sister are from Tennessee. We killed three of them bank robbers, but the last one got away, and he was the fella that set the ambush. We're all sorry as hell about it, but that doesn't make it our fault."

Elias glared at Ruff, then wobbled over to a water trough. Dropping to his knees, he dipped his entire upper body in the trough and came up sputtering. He had long, white hair and a handlebar mustache to match. Slicking back both, he shook himself like a wet dog and tramped over to his son's body. Ruff saw the man's shoulder's sag as he marshaled his deepest inner reserves.

"I'm takin' my son home," he said to no one in particular.

"Here," the mayor said, stepping forward, "let me help you load up Charlie's body."

"Don't you touch him!" Elias screeched, hand blanketing the butt of his six-gun.

Morton recoiled so fast he tripped over the edge of the boardwalk and spilled onto his back. No one laughed, and most also retreated, watching as the old man dragged his son over to his buckboard and struggled to dump Charlie's body into the bed of his wagon. Without another word, Elias Benson climbed into his wagon and drove away.

"Do you think he meant it?" Dixie finally asked, breaking a long silence.

"Meant what?" the marshal asked.

"Meant it when he said he'd kill you."

"Oh, I expect that he did mean it. He may change his mind after a few weeks of mourning, but I doubt it."

Ruff massaged his stinging knuckles. "Be a hell of a thing, always watching your back."

"I won't have to do that, should Elias come to kill me," Gus said. "He's no back-shooter; he'll face me man to man."

"Is he good with a gun?"

"He's good with a rifle," Gus said, "but only fair with a pistol."

The marshal ordered the other bodies to be taken to the mortician's office, and then he said, "You and your sister would be wise to put distance between yourselves and old Elias."

"You take his threat seriously then, don't you?" Dixie said, not trying to hide her concern.

"I do," the marshal admitted. "And there's been more than enough killing to go around in the last two days. I'd not want to see your names added to the list bound for our cemetery."

"Let's go," Dixie pleaded.

"Marshal Gus, are you really going to go after that gang of bank robbers?"

"You bet I am. I'll be leaving just as soon as I can get a posse deputized."

"Good luck," Ruff said, certain that the marshal was going to need it and wondering if he was fit enough to go on a long trackdown.

Ruff and Dixie shook the old lawman's hand and left to collect their mares. They were both anxious to ride and put the bloody memory of Rio Paso far behind. It took some time to get the mares roped together again and buy a few supplies for the trail, but at last it was time to go.

"Mr. Ballou?"

"Yes?" Ruff asked, turning to face a very worried and upset mayor.

Morton cleared his throat, then hemmed and hawed for a few moments before he blurted, "Marshal Gus can't get anyone else to volunteer to ride with him as his deputy."

This announcement shouldn't have come as a surprise, but it did, and while Ruff tried to digest it, Dixie said, "Then why don't you ride with him?"

"Because I'd be more a hindrance than a help. I can't shoot nor ride a horse worth beans, Miss Ballou. And everyone that can has begged off."

"So what has that got to do with us?"

"Well, I'm coming to that directly. You see, I was so upset when I realized that Gus was going alone and in bad health that I hastily called a town council meeting. There's only the five of us, and we've decided to offer a five hundred dollar reward—on top of the two thousand that has already been pledged by Mr. Rudd—for the capture of that last bank robber."

"And what about his fellow ambushers?" Ruff asked.

"Well," the mayor hedged, suddenly dropping his eyes, "naturally, we want them to be brought back for justice, too. But something is better than nothing so even that one bank robber would be a welcome justice and an important lesson to anyone else not to rob a bank in Rio Paso."

"Why are you telling us this?"

"Mr. Ballou, we want you to join the marshal."

"No!" Dixie exclaimed. "This isn't our fight. We've already killed three of the four. Isn't that enough?"

Morton nodded vigorously. "Sure. I mean . . . it ought to be, but the town council is real worried about Gus. He's not up to a hard chase with his heart condition."

Ruff blinked. "Heart condition?"

"That's right. Oh, I know that he looks stronger than a Missouri mule, but he's got a bad heart."

"Then he shouldn't go," Ruff said.

"I know that and so do we, but he will anyway. That's why someone has got to help him. Someone who has proven they can handle a gun and maybe track a little better than Gus. That someone has to be you, Mr. Ballou."

Ruff looked to Dixie, who shook her head adamantly. "No."

"Sure wish your brother would reconsider. Otherwise, Marshal Gus hasn't much of a chance, has he?"

Ruff looked to Dixie. "The mayor is right. It's too much to expect of one man."

"Or two!"

"Dixie, fifteen hundred dollars would go a long way toward buying us a big piece of property up near Denver so we could start building right away."

"Please don't," Dixie begged. "We've been through so much already to get this far. We've earned a chance to build again, Ruff."

Ruff understood Dixie's fears. If he died, she'd be all alone with a lot of very valuable horses to protect.

"All right," Ruff said with more than a little bit of reluctance.

The mayor's thin shoulders sagged. "Can't say as I blame you, young fella. But Gus has long been a friend of mine, and he deserves better than to be shot down by a bunch of outlaws."

"Yeah," Ruff said, "he does. But I'm thinking that he will at least take a few with him."

"That's true, but it won't be much consolation to his daughters."

"Daughters?"

"Yeah," Morton said, "one in Albuquerque and the other in Santa Fe. They're about your age, too. It's going to be hard on 'em when they hear he rode out alone and got killed because no one would help."

"Stop it!" Dixie said angrily. "If you think that you can make my brother feel some kind of guilt, you're wrong. This isn't our fight and we're leaving."

Morton wrung his bony hands. "Yes, Miss Ballou," he said, dipping his pointy chin up and down, "I expect that is the smart thing to do."

Ruff could tell by the mayor's tone of voice that he might think it smart, but also a tragedy. So, on impulse, he said, "How much money does the city council actually have?"

The question caught Morton off guard. "Huh?"

"I asked how much this town really can pay—how bad do you want those ambushers?"

Morton toed the dirt, hemmed and hawed, and then he said, "Well, I guess we could go two thousand."

"Two thousand plus the five hundred?"

Morton struggled for a moment, then he gulped, "Ah-yep."

"Then I'm in," Ruff said.

"No!" Dixie cried.

But Ruff's mind was made up. Dixie would have to stay to protect the mares from being stolen, and he would ride out with the old marshal. Maybe they'd get lucky, but even at the worst, they wouldn't get drunk and be dumb enough to blunder into another ambush.

SIX

It didn't take Ruff long to pack his gear and saddle High Fire. Dixie was angry and upset, but kept her silence.

"Well," Ruff said, "I guess that I'm all ready to go." He dug into his pockets and pulled out most of his cash. "You take this and find yourself a good room with board."

"How long will you stick this out?" Dixie asked quietly.

"What do you mean?"

"I mean, what if the bank robber and his friends have headed on down to Texas? Just how far will you and Marshal Gus go to bring those men to justice?"

"I won't go that far," Ruff promised. "I'll be back inside a month."

"A month!"

"Dixie, there's twenty-five hundred dollars at stake as well as bringing those men to justice."

"I heard that dying man say that there were six or seven ambushers. Those are terrible odds."

"We'll be careful. The marshal is an old hand at this sort of thing, and while he might not be in good health, he's not going to let us make any fatal mistakes."

"There's no talking you out of this, is there?"

"I'm afraid not." Ruff scowled. "I'm more worried about that damned Bob Justin pestering you than I am about getting into some kind of trouble that I can't handle."

"I'll be fine."

Ruff expected this was true. Dixie was young, but she had a lot of character and determination. If Bob Justin tried to pull any shenanigans, he was in for a rude awakening because Dixie could be a wildcat when she got her back up.

"All right," Ruff said, "we're just going to have to trust each other to handle things. You've got a big responsibility watching over the mares."

"I'll find a cheaper place to keep them," Dixie said. "A pasture that won't eat up what money we have left for a board bill."

"Our decisions always seem to come down to not having enough money," Ruff said with resignation. "But if the marshal and I are successful, we'll finally have enough to make a fresh start."

"You just be careful," Dixie said, "and I'm not going to sit around here and twiddle my thumbs while you're gone off with Marshal Gus."

"What does that mean?"

"It means I have to believe that you and the marshal are going to earn that reward. That being the case, I might as well look at some land that would do for a horse ranch."

"Are you going to do it with that cow-eyed cattle rancher?"

"Maybe."

Ruff ground his teeth with exasperation. "Dixie, I don't like Bob Justin and neither does the marshal. So why don't you just, well . . ."

"Just what?" Dixie demanded to know. "Work in the cafe or the hotel? You know that I'm not suited for waiting on people. I'm best with horses, just like you are. So what exactly am I supposed to do for the next month?"

Ruff thought hard. "Maybe you could let the word out that you are available to train some local horses."

Dixie scoffed. "Oh sure! I can just imagine how eager the cowboys and ranchers in these parts would be to hire a fifteen-year-old girl from Tennessee. They'd consider the mere suggestion an insult."

"All right, then we can think of something else."

"I'm listening."

Ruff chewed on that a moment and said, "Maybe you could race a mare and sell her based on the speed she shows over the best of the local horses."

"Are you telling me that you want to take both of our stallions?"

"No, just High Fire. But I'd rather you didn't race High Man, given his age and the hard miles we've put on him of late."

"He's still fast and strong."

"Race one of the mares. That sorrel with the blaze on her face and the three white stockings ought to be able to run like a high prairie wind."

"We'll see," Dixie said. "A girl has to do what she has to do to survive."

"Meaning?"

"Just what I said. All I know is that this morning, we'd agreed to ride for Denver; now you're off for a month and God only knows what will happen if you get killed."

Ruff ground his teeth because, once in a great while, Dixie got herself in such a state that it was useless to try and talk good sense to her. She was in such a state now.

"I'd better go," Ruff said, mounting his young Thoroughbred stallion. "Dixie, I swear that I'll be back within a month and we'll have enough money to buy the kind of land we want—either here or up in Colorado. Might be we can even buy a spread that's already developed real nice with a house, barn, and corrals so that all we'll have to do is lay out a few pastures and a warm-up track."

"I'd rather we tried to earn the money racing our horses, just like our family has always done, rather than you riding off after a bunch of killers."

Ruff didn't have anything else to say about that. He knew that Dixie was right, that he should have stuck with their original plan. But the marshal needed help. Besides, the ambushers had shed too much blood and they couldn't be allowed to escape.

"So long, Dixie," Ruff said quietly as he reined away. "I'll return as soon as I can."

Dixie caught up with him before High Fire had walked ten feet. "Ruff, dammit! You'd better come back or I'll never speak to you again!"

A smile replaced Ruff's grim expression, and he chuckled. "You got a deal," he said, reaching down to squeeze his kid sister's hand. "I promise that I'll be back."

Ruff found the marshal in his office preoccupied with inspecting a sawed-off, double-barreled shotgun. When Gus turned and saw Ruff, he said, "I thought you and that sassy sister of yours had already left for Denver."

"She's stayin', but I'm goin' with you, Marshal Gus."

The lawman didn't look up and his expression didn't change as he finished his inspection. He reloaded the shotgun and snapped its breech closed. "What made you decide to change your mind. The big reward?"

"That's part of it," Ruff said, not wanting to tell the lawman that Morton had also used the worry of a heart condition and two pretty young daughters to seal his argument.

"Twenty-five hundred dollars is a lot of money," the marshal said, "and I told Morton that I will personally shoot the bunch of them fellas that offered it if they should decide to change their minds."

"And the mayor said?"

"Morton is a man of his word," Gus answered. "I know he doesn't look like much, but I've seen him angry, and he carries a derringer which he will use if forced to the act."

"I see."

The marshal laid the shotgun across the crook of his arm and scooped up his saddlebags. "Are you riding that big young stallion?"

"Yes."

"Then I'll take Jeremiah's horse as well as my own. Between the two of them, they'll have an easier time of keeping me abreast of you tall youngsters. Even with two horses, I expect we'll have to hump to match your pace."

"Where do you want to start?"

"At that box canyon near Little Alder Creek," Gus said without hesitation. "I figure that's where we can pick up their tracks. They won't be expecting anyone to follow them."

"Then let's go."

For the first time, the marshal really looked at Ruff. "Are you sure you want a piece of this?"

"Even split down the middle, it's a sizable reward."

"And that's all?"

Ruff inhaled. "No," he said, "there's a matter of justice that needs to be meted out. Jeremiah died hard, and I don't feel right about letting his killers get away scot-free."

"Good!" Marshal Gus smiled. He reached into his desk and selected a full bottle of whiskey. "You can have this one for the trail."

"No, thanks."

"Then I'll bring it along to warm my bones at night," Gus said. "But don't worry, I won't get drunk and make the same kind of mistake that Charlie Benson and those boys made."

"I'm counting on that," Ruff said a moment before he followed the marshal outside.

Gus pulled up short on the boardwalk, caught by a sudden idea. "Say, has that sister of yours found a boardinghouse yet?"

"No."

"And I don't suppose that you have a lot of money."

Ruff had no idea what the marshal was angling toward. "That's right."

"Then she can move into my office."

"What?"

"Why not?"

"Kee-rist," Ruff grumbled. "That's about the dumbest idea I've heard of in a long, long time."

"Well hear me out, dammit! I could leave her the key and everything. The city don't pay me much, but they do allow for three meals a day and old Wong Woo puts on a pretty decent feed. Your sister could sleep here and eat for free."

"I doubt that the city council would share your spirit of generosity," Ruff said with a shake of his head.

"I'll talk to Morton before we leave. He owns the general store directly across the street. I have to get us some provisions anyway. You go talk to your obstinate sister and remind her that if Bob Longhorn Justin gets to be too much of a bother, she can protect her honor by locking herself in the jail cell and hanging onto the key."

Ruff threw the man a quizzical look, sure he was being joshed, but the marshal's expression was serious. "All right," Ruff said, "you talk to Morton and I'll pay a quick visit to my sister. But I still think it's a crazy damn thing to do."

"Not if you're about broke and this turns into a long trackdown."

Ruff remounted his horse and went to find Dixie. When he told her about the offer, she stared at him like he was daft.

"Don't look at me that way," Ruff said. "It was the marshal's idea, not mine."

"You must have agreed or you wouldn't be here."

"The marshal's office has a roof, a floor, and a bed. Even better, the free rent includes three square meals from Wong Woo's Chinese cafe. I don't think we can afford to turn it down."

"I've never even eaten Chinese food. What is it?"

"Lots of rice and stuff, I think."

"Yuck!"

"The marshal says its great."

Dixie looked disgusted. "And what am I supposed to do if there is trouble?"

"What do you mean?"

"I mean," Dixie said, placing her hands on her narrow hips, "what if someone gets drunk and goes on a tear and then needs to be jailed?"

"Hmmm," Ruff mused, "I'll have to admit that I hadn't thought about that."

"Well, you should have! And what happens if there is another bank robbery while you two are away and more people are shot? Am I supposed to become the marshal, deputize everyone, and go after them with my posse?"

Ruff was beginning to get annoyed. "Listen, I'm sorry that I even brought the idea up."

"You ought to be."

"If you change your mind, the mayor has the key," Ruff said before reining High Fire around and riding back to find Marshal Gus. Dixie could sure be difficult, and there were a lot of times when Ruff wished that she'd learn to take a more open attitude about things.

The marshal was over at Rio Paso's combination livery and blacksmith shop saddling his horse and packing the one that had belonged to young Jeremiah. Marshal Gus also had a blacksmith at work tacking on a loose shoe.

"I'll be ready in just a minute," Gus said. "No sense in getting a few miles out and losing a shoe."

"Maybe I'd better have him replace my stallion's shoes as well," Ruff said after dismounting. "They've been on since we left Texas almost two months ago."

"I can't help you," the blacksmith answered, glancing up. "I don't mess with stallions. Been hurt a couple of times, and I won't fool with 'em."

"This stallion is a gentleman," Ruff explained, picking up High Fire's right forefoot as easy as you please. "See."

"Maybe he's a gentleman for you 'cause you own him and he knows you'll rap his beans if he gets rambunctious. But he don't know me, and I'm not touching him. I don't trust a stud horse as far as I can throw 'em."

"Then I'll do it myself," Ruff said, deciding that any blacksmith so worrisome probably wasn't very good anyway. "I've shod a lot of horses and prefer my own work. Can I use your forge and anvil?"

"You know what you're doin'? That anvil of mine is the best that money can buy. Sent for it all the way to Boston. I don't want you banging it up."

Ruff didn't know what else an anvil was for if not to be "banged up." But he nodded and said, "I won't."

Ruff then proceeded to tie on an extra leather apron and go to work. He pulled off High Fire's badly worn shoes and then used the nippers, a knife, and a rasp as if he shod horses every day of his life. His father had taught all the boys to use a forge and an anvil, and Ruff quickly had the shoes shaped and fitted proper. When he tacked them on hot, it caused a familiar white, acrid smoke to burn his nostrils.

"You do good work," the blacksmith said with grudging admiration.

"How much do I owe you for the use of your tools, the shoes, and the nails?"

"A dollar will be fine."

Ruff paid the blacksmith and turned to Gus. "I guess we're finally ready?"

"As ready as we'll ever be," Gus said, hauling himself into the saddle.

As they rode out into the street, the mayor came bustling over. "I was able to win the city council's approval on that girl using your office, Gus. But they weren't too happy about old Wong Woo having to provide her with free meals."

"Tough," Gus snapped. "That girl shot one of the bank robbers dead. Givin' her free room and board ain't much in the way of payment while her brother and I follow the outlaw trail."

"I don't think she'll even accept the offer," Ruff told both men. "Dixie sure didn't take to the idea of living in a marshal's office."

"I ain't that dirty," Gus said, looking somewhat offended.

"No," Ruff agreed, "but Dixie still wasn't very excited about the prospect."

"Strange girl you got for a sister. No place safer for her to be than locked in my cell and she's got the keys."

As they trotted off, Ruff guessed this was true. And it was encouraging the way that the people of Rio Paso came outside to line the street and wish them a safe and speedy return. It gave Ruff a real nice feeling until he remembered that not a single damned one of them had the guts to be deputized by the marshal on what might prove to be a long and bloody trail.

SEVEN

They rode steadily through what remained of the day. High Fire was plenty eager to travel, but the marshal's little buckskin and the horse he'd inherited from Jeremiah were just not up to the mark. Jeremiah's horse was a good enough animal, but it had traveled a lot of hard miles during the past few days, and it was clearly played out. The buckskin, Ruff decided at a glance, was just about everything in a horse that you would try to breed out. It was jug-headed, runty, and cow-hocked. The marshal said that the animal rode like an ore wagon, and Ruff imagined that was true.

"I never did like riding horses," Gus complained that night when they made camp about fifteen miles south of Little Alder Creek. "All my grown years, I have tried to avoid them whenever possible."

Ruff shrugged. "It would seem to me that they're sort of necessary in your line of work."

"Yeah, but the damn things cost too much, they eat too much, and they often go lame. They've no loyalty to a man and will leave him stranded given half a chance."

Ruff pulled his saddle off High Fire's back. "Marshal Gus, you and I take opposite views. To me, a horse is a thing of pure beauty. If you break them right and train them gentle, they're as loyal as dogs. They don't ask for much except a scratch behind the ears and a bellyful of grass."

"Which they immediately turn into big clumps of ripe green apples that draw flies."

Ruff ignored the comment and continued. "If you grain horses, they'll love you forever and carry you until they drop. To watch a horse run, tail up, nostrils extended, mane flying . . . well, that's to see God's most beautiful creature in motion."

"Ha!" Gus scoffed. "Mister, you and I haven't been riding the same kind of animals."

Ruff glanced over at the marshal's buckskin. "That's for sure."

"I like mules better than horses," Gus said, flopping down on the grass and lacing his fingers behind his head. "And dogs and even cats. But not horses."

"Marshal, you sound like an unlikely candidate for becoming a lawman."

"I was. The truth is, like most people, I just fell into this low-payin' profession. But that's real common. How many people really go on to do what they planned with their lives?"

"I mean to," Ruff said. "Horses are my life, just as they have been for my whole family."

"I was a mule skinner. Mules are smart, horses are dumb, and don't be surprised if you wind up bein' a damn lawyer, blacksmith, or farmer."

"Not a chance."

"Well, I sure didn't expect to become no marshal until the day I saw one gunned down by a cowardly back-shooter in a little jerk-water town called Dugan, Texas."

"Never heard of it."

"Burned down about four years ago. Even the folks that lived there said good riddance. Anyway, the back-shooter was drunk and he was a cowboy without honor or skill. The marshal had been forced to whip the cowboy with his pistol and arrest him the previous night for roughing up a dance-hall girl. Next day, the cowboy's friends made his bail and the fella got drunk again and sneaked up on the marshal. Shot him twice right between the shoulder blades."

"And you jumped in with both feet."

"Like you and your sister when them bank-robbin' sonsabitches came barrelin' through your horses, I felt compelled to take action."

"Sometimes," Ruff said, "you act before you even have time to think."

"Yeah," Gus agreed. "When I saw the marshal of Dugan fall, I shouted a curse at the murderin' cowboy. He whirled around and took a wild shot in my direction. That was the first time I'd ever been shot at, and I was so scared that I ran about forty feet before I stopped, turned around, and drew my own six-gun."

"And you killed the cowboy."

"Nope. I was just a mule skinner and wanted no part of the fight, but when I saw the cowboy step over the marshal's body like he was nothin' more'n a log, then swagger over to his horse and start to ride away, then something snapped. I ran over and told the cowboy he was under arrest."

"That was bold. Were you scared?"

"The barrel of my gun was shaking like a preacher's finger!"

The marshal grinned at himself. "The cowboy laughed in my face, and that made me so mad that I got rattled and shot him in the foot."

"The foot?"

"Didn't mean to. My gun accidentally went off. Could have shot myself in the foot just as easily. Anyway, the cowboy commenced to dancing around and around and howling like a scalded dog. I put my gun away and punched him in the jaw. He dropped and kept on howling, so I took his gun, grabbed his cartridge belt, and dragged him over to the marshal's office."

Gus chuckled. "Course, I didn't have a key. It was on the marshal's body, and there was a great deal of confusion among folks. Many of them were afraid that the cowboy's friends would raze the town."

"But you weren't afraid, were you?"

"Sure I was! I got my mule-skinner friends together, and since there was no one else callin' himself a lawman in Dugan, I deputized the whole damn bunch of 'em. That afternoon, we almost had ourselves a war between the cowboys and them Texas mule whackers."

"What kept the bullets from flying?"

"I sent for the judge, and when they said he was afraid to try the case, we all took a vote and hanged the back-shooter from a barn's rafter."

Ruff shook his head. "Just like that?"

"Yep. And you know what?"

"What?"

"Once those cowboys saw their friend swinging from a rope with the sign I'd tied around his neck reading, 'BACK-SHOOTER,' they just decided it wasn't worth the fight."

"I'll bet the town of Dugan was happy."

"Happy, yes," Marshal Gus said, "but not one bit grateful. They asked us all to leave, but about a week later, the fella they hired to replace their dead marshal was killed while showing off with his own gun."

"He shot himself?"

"That's right. Was a fast draw, only he forgot to clear leather. Bullet traveled down his leg and musta hit an artery, because the poor fool bled to death."

"And they came and asked you to take his place."

"Nope. I freighted for about another six months before I arrived back in Dugan. By that time, the riffraff had taken over the town and the people were desperate enough to ask me to help them out. And this I was happy to do because two of my mules had gotten the colic and died, so I was out of the business and in bad need of a paycheck."

"And then you stuck to being a lawman?"

"Nope. I quit Dugan and tried to ranch. Failing at that, I ran a saloon, and I even failed at that enterprise, though there are some who will tell you it isn't possible out here in the West. Next, I opened a cafe in Dugan, but rotted meat poisoned my customers and they almost hanged me from the same barn rafter I'd hanged the back-shooter from!"

"If nothing else, you've had an interesting life," Ruff said in wonder.

"Oh, hell," the marshal said with a wave of his hand, "the best part was becoming a buffalo hunter, but that didn't last too long, and when the business got down to pickin' bones and sellin' em, I decided the only thing that I'd been any good at was that one time in Dugan, when I appointed myself marshal."

"I understand that you have a couple of daughters."

The marshal's eyes snapped. "Who told you that?"

"Mayor Morton."

"That skinny son of a bitch talks too much."

"He said that your daughters live in Albuquerque and Santa Fe."

Gus was silent for a few moments. "They're a couple of real beauties, all right. One is married and has two fine boys."

"And the other?"

A stab of pain flashed across the marshal's wrinkled face. "She's had bad luck with men. Just a string of real awful luck. Her first husband was a marshal like me, but he got killed. She married again, and the second husband turned out to be a drunk and a wife beater. I had to go over there and straighten Willy out. Almost cost me my job when word got back to Rio Paso what a thorough reeducatin' job I'd done."

"I see."

The sheriff's fists knotted. "So does Willy, and I doubt he'll ever beat another human being again, because I left him in such bad shape that it's all he can do to feed hisself. Course, my daughter got mad, and now I'm the one that was wrong. She won't speak to me. Can you imagine that?"

"Women can be blind when it comes to their husbands," Ruff said. "But, in my experience, time heals a lot of things. Besides, what else were you supposed to do other than knock some good sense and a gentleman's manners into the fella?"

Gus shrugged his round shoulders. "I guess maybe hold Willy's hands and have a friendly man-to-man talk with him instead of breaking his hands and a whole lot of other bones besides."

Gus sat up and rolled a cigarette. "But that's enough about my family. What else did Morton tell you about me?"

"Nothing much."

"Morton likes to talk, so I doubt that you're tellin' me the truth, though I ain't exactly sayin' you're an out-and-out liar."

Ruff hedged, not wanting to get Morton into trouble but not comfortable with a lie. "The mayor said something about your health."

"My health!" Gus swore passionately. "Why that skinny, beady-eyed little weasel! I'm strong as a mule and have the constitution of an ox! Morton has always envied my size and strength, and that's why he says such foolishness."

"Whatever you say, Marshal Gus."

The marshal ground his teeth in anger. "It appears that I'm going to have to take that little pecker-neck down a peg or two when we get back to Rio Paso."

"He's just concerned about you."

Gus made the sound of a mule passing wind. "If our mayor was really so damned concerned, why didn't he volunteer to join us!"

"He says he can't shoot straight or ride a horse," Ruff offered. "Besides that, he's the mayor and probably feels he ought to stick to home."

"The mayor of Rio Paso don't do diddly-squat! Just has a breakfast meeting once or twice a year. Oh yeah, and he has the dubious honor of presiding over our annual Fourth of July celebrations."

"Well," Ruff said, "Morton does care about you, and I suspect that he's a good friend."

"The little squawk is all mouth," the marshal grumped. "A man don't need friends like that tellin' big windies about his health and such."

The marshal's eyes bored into Ruff. "Did Morton say anything else about me?"

"Nope."

Gus was satisfied enough to drop the matter. He stretched, groaned, and said, "Well, you may consider yourself a real horseman, but I'll keep up with whatever pace you want to set."

"Is that a fact?"

"Yep. Actually, I thought we weren't pushing it hard enough today, but I didn't want to exhaust that big stallion of yours. With them long, skinny legs, I expect he'll break down before another week passes."

Ruff took instant offense, but he didn't take the bait. Gus looked played out, and the last thing he and the marshal needed was to get angry with each another. So, instead, Ruff tended to the horses, then gathered firewood and generally made the camp while the marshal nodded off and began to snore.

After sundown, the marshal awoke from his nap to the smell of coffee, beef, and beans cooking. He helped himself to a plate of food and ate like a starved wolf.

"Ruff, thought it pains me to admit it, you ain't an altogether bad cook."

"Thanks."

The marshal looked as pleased as if he'd landed a big fish. "Well then, that being agreed upon, you can be our cook and dishwasher."

Ruff shook his head with an emphatic wag that left no room for compromise. "Marshal Gus, I will do the cooking, but if you eat off a plate, you clean it yourself."

"Hump!" the marshal grunted. "Just my luck to get stuck on a long manhunt with a grouchy bastard like you."

Ruff finished his plate, then wiped it clean with grass. He went to check the hobbles on High Fire and spend a little time with the young stallion before he bedded down for the night. Gus lay back down on his bedroll and began to snore so loud that the horses stopped grazing and snorted with alarm.

Ruff spoke some soothing horse talk to them, and they went back to grazing in the starlight. Ruff turned back to study the marshal. Gus was an irascible old man who should have retired long ago. He was too damned old to be gallivanting around after a bunch of cutthroats and ambushers, and certainly had no business doing it by his lonesome. It was, Ruff knew, a real good thing that he had decided to come along despite Dixie's objections. He just hoped that girl was going to be all right without his company and protection.

EIGHT

His name was Roscoe Conklin, and he was a short, wizen-faced man in his late sixties. He was rail-thin, dirty, and chewed a great wad of tarry tobacco which dribbled through the mostly gaps in his teeth, to river down the stubble of his chin and drip steadily onto his round-toed shoes. Dixie thought the shoes were very disgusting.

"Ain't you getting hungry, little Missy?"

"Hungry?"

"Why, sure," Roscoe said, loosing a fine spray of tobacco that kept Dixie at two-arms' distance. "You can't stay here at my livery all night. Why don't you just take the marshal's offer and hole up in his jail?"

"That just doesn't seem very proper."

"Proper, hell! It's better'n sleeping in some alley or payin' good money to a boarding room." Roscoe winked. "Whatever money you have had better come to me for feedin' all your pretty racin' mares."

"You'll be paid," Dixie vowed. "Tomorrow, I'll find a job."

"Where?" Roscoe demanded, leaning forward with sudden interest on his empty horseshoe keg.

"Maybe you could use some help," Dixie said hopefully.

"Nope. I got thirty-two horses boarded here, about half of which you own and are goin' through my hay like locust through a cornfield. I sure don't need no further expenses."

"I can break horses. Do you have any bad ones?"

"Nope. I give my outlaws to the local Indians, and that way they never try and steal my good horses."

"What do they do with them?"

"Break 'em or eat 'em."

Her eyes widened. "You'd sell horses to someone who might eat them!"

"When I sell a horse, it ain't none of my business what becomes of it," Roscoe explained. "Now, that don't mean I'd sit here all day and watch a man beat a horse to death. No, siree! But neither would I interfere if a man wants to bang his nag around a little so that she knows who is the boss."

"You Westerners sure have a hard attitude about animals. Don't you know horses respond better to patience and kindness?"

Roscoe giggled, a high, womanish giggle that made him sound a little crazy.

"Kindness? Why, Missy, kindness ain't in the vocabulary of the Western cowboy or bronc buster. A horse is made for carryin' a man or pulling a wagon or a plow. That's all."

"Not true! My horses are bred for speed. For winning horse races, and their owners nice, fat purses. Haven't you ever gone to a horse race and bet money?"

"Why, sure! I've won, and I've lost. But I never shot the horse that lost and I never kissed the winner."

Dixie just did not understand this kind of thinking. Digging into her pockets, she pulled out a dollar, thinking that she had to get something to eat.

"Why, thank you!" Roscoe said, his hand plucking the greenback away quicker than a chicken gobbles a grub. "This'll pay for half of today's feed. Got any more?"

"We have a deal," Dixie snapped. "You agreed to wait until my brother and Marshal Gus returned to claim the reward money. Your boarding bill comes out of that."

"Yeah, and if they don't return, you'd better start selling some of them tall mares in a big hurry, 'cause this ain't no charity, Missy. You're a real sweetie, fer sure. But the only green around here I want to see is that of the almighty government dollar."

Dixie glanced up and down the street. "Here comes the mayor."

They both watched as Morton shuffled up toward them in his loose-limbed way. The mayor removed his hat to reveal a receding hairline. "Afternoon, Roscoe. Miss Ballou."

The liveryman grunted something, and Dixie smiled. "Afternoon."

"The marshal's office is cleaned up real nice. I had Wong Woo's daughter see to it. You got clean sheets and everything, Miss Ballou."

Dixie frowned and came to her feet. "I just don't know about this. I was thinking that you might try and talk Roscoe into letting me sleep in his hayloft so I could stay near my mares. Tomorrow, next day at the latest, I'm sure that I could find a job and—"

"Now, Miss Ballou," Morton said patiently. "As the mayor of Rio Paso, I feel a certain . . . responsibility toward your welfare. Especially considering that we don't have the marshal in town and that makes us all very nervous."

"This doesn't look like a very wild town to me," Dixie said, glancing up and down the street.

"It can be plenty wild," the mayor said. "Isn't that right, Roscoe?"

"It can when the boys come into town for a payday. What is today, Morton?"

"Friday."

"Then the cowboys will get paid and be in tomorrow."

"That's right." The mayor dipped his chin up and down. "So you see, Miss Ballou, we want you to be safe in our jail. Also, the meals are going to be delivered, and if you are not there to eat, then the food'll be tossed out to the dogs."

"Why don't you just tell Mr. Woo to stop bringing the food over until the marshal returns?"

"You don't understand the Oriental's mind, young lady. He doesn't speak our language, and he thinks altogether different. What Wong Woo is sure of is that he gets paid by the town to deliver meals every day. And if we tried to make him understand that he is not to deliver those meals, he would get very upset."

"A Chinaman," Roscoe interjected, "is a thing to behold when he really gets upset. Wong Woo took up a meat cleaver one time and nearly beheaded some fool who refused to pay for his supper."

"Oh," Dixie said.

"So you see," Morton said with an understanding smile, "it would make things much easier if only you'd cooperate and do as Marshal Gus asked."

"All right," Dixie said with resignation. "But I want the keys to the front door as well as the keys to the jail cell."

"Of course."

"And what if someone gets rowdy and needs to be arrested?"

Morton looked to Roscoe and then back to Dixie. He shrugged his thin shoulders and said, "I don't know what will happen in that case. I need to discuss it with the town council first thing next Monday morning."

"Why wait?" Dixie asked with a frown.

"Because that's when we meet each month," Morton explained as if the answer were perfectly clear.

Dixie gave up. The next obvious question to ask was what the town would do if the cowboys hoo-rahhed Rio Paso tomorrow night. But that was the logical question, and logic seemed to have nothing to do with the way things were done in this part of the Rio Grande Valley.

"Here are the keys," Morton said, handing her a ring. "The big one is to the jail cell, the medium one to the front door, and the little one fits into the rifle rack."

Dixie took the keys. "And are the meals delivered?"

"Mr. Woo will arrive morning, noon, and night with a steaming tray that will make your mouth water."

"Mostly rice, I'll bet."

"And some beef, pork, and vegetables."

Dixie made a face. "I don't think that I'm going to gain any weight while I'm hanging around Rio Paso."

"You might be surprised," the mayor said. "Wong Woo started out with only one or two of us eating at his place. But as the word got around, even the cowboys started coming in to sample his cooking. He's built up quite a following and put one of our local cafes out of business. His food is cheap, wholesome, and clean."

"All right," Dixie said. "It seems that I've little choice, and I am hungry enough to eat most anything."

The mayor beamed, and Roscoe spit with a smile. "You're makin' the right choice, Missy."

Dixie didn't consider that she had any choice. Ruff was out there somewhere risking his life to win a badly needed reward and to bring some assassins to justice. The least she could do was to try and not run up any more of a bill for herself than was necessary until Ruff returned.

"I'd appreciate it if you'd let the word out that I am a very good horse breaker and trainer."

"Not much of that kind of business around Rio Paso," the mayor said. "It's all done on the ranches scattered around in the hills and up in the big valleys off the Rio Grande."

"But there are plenty of people in town who have horses," Dixie argued. "Some of them must also have behavioral problems."

"If they do," Morton said, "they sell those horses to Roscoe and he knows how to get rid of them."

"So I've heard."

And with that, Dixie took the marshal's keys and started up the street.

The marshal's office had been cleaned up real nice, and, most important, there was fresh linen on the small bed that was tucked behind a pair of big oak filing cabinets. The marshal's desk was littered with correspondence and wanted posters; ammunition and a disassembled six-gun were neatly laid out on an oily towel on top of the desk. Dixie gathered up the pistol with its springs and mechanisms, then opened a drawer, but it was filled with whiskey bottles, some empty, others partially full. There were also empty packets that appeared to have held some kind of medicinal powders.

Dixie paused a moment, her brow furrowing with concern. The very last thing that Ruff needed was to be riding into trouble with an unhealthy and hard-drinking lawman.

A knock on the door brought Dixie up short. She laid the disassembled Colt revolver down and went to the door to see the Chinaman. He was a dapper man, all smiles, who was dressed in a shiny black outfit with red dragons embroidered on its sleeves. Wong Woo wore his hair in a long, braided queue, and his face was shiny with perspiration. He looked very gentle, even serene. It was hard to imagine that this man really could go after someone with a meat cleaver.

"Bring good food, Missy," he said, extending a covered tray in Dixie's direction.

She took a whiff of the food and realized that she was famished. "Thank you, Mr. Woo. My name is Dixie."

He grinned, and his head bobbed up and down several times. "Hope likee, Missy," he said with a smile before he bowed and silently retreated across the street, seeming to glide on a pair of black, lacquered sandals.

When Dixie laid the tray on the marshal's desk and opened the lid, the aroma was almost overpowering. She leaned forward and inhaled the pork and rice, with its celery and delicate sauces. Dixie picked up a little cup without a handle and sipped at the tea, with its refreshing mint taste. She used her fingers to pluck up delicious morsels of chicken, pork, and crunchy noodles.

"My oh my," she whispered, closing her eyes and flopping down into the marshal's scarred old office chair. Moments later, she was gobbling up everything and wishing there was more.

That night, Dixie stayed up late, rummaging around in the office, reading wanted posters, and getting a feel for the character of Marshal Gus. She found a pair of daguerreotypes of pretty young women posing with handsome young men, and she wondered whether she was looking at Gus's sons or his daughters. There was a worn Bible in the upper right-hand drawer, with passages well marked, and several letters that she would never have opened.

Dixie decided that the marshal was exactly as he seemed—a good and conscientious man but one that needed to retire and take better care of his health.

"Maybe this reward money means even more to Marshal Gus than it does to Ruff and me," she said, blowing out the kerosene lamp and stretching out to sleep.

NINE

Dixie awoke early the next morning and dressed quickly. It felt strange sleeping in a marshal's office, and when she looked at the naked bars of the spartan jail cell, she wondered at the stories that must have unfolded here over the years. There were at least seven or eight rifles in the rack, and Dixie would have bet that Marshal Gus had been called upon to use every one of them from time to time.

As soon as she was ready, Dixie hurried outside, locked the office, and went over to Roscoe Conklin's livery. She was the only one on the street at this early hour, and the sun was just beginning to burn the eastern horizon. The moment her mares recognized Dixie, they whinnied a greeting. A few minutes later, Dixie was tossing the Thoroughbreds their breakfast and the sun was still glued to the eastern mountaintops.

Dixie loved this time of the morning, when the day was fresh and crisp. She remembered her Tennessee childhood and how her father had loved to get up early and go out to greet each new day and silently commune with his beloved Thoroughbreds. In his younger years, Justin Ballou would saddle and gallop his horses around the family racetrack, glorying in the rising sun and the brisk way that the Thoroughbreds felt at that early hour. And even in his later years, Justin had thoroughly enjoyed watching Dixie and her brothers exercise the mares and stallions while he clocked their workouts.

Dixie leaned on the top rail of the corral to watch the mares eat. She smiled to remember those wonderful times before the Civil War had destroyed everything that she and her family held dear.

"You fallin' asleep already, Missy?"

Dixie turned to see Roscoe. The man was only half-dressed, pulling his suspenders over his narrow shoulders and stuffing his dirty shirt into a pair of baggy brown pants. Even at this early hour, Roscoe's cheek was bulging like that of a foraging squirrel, and he spat a stream of tobacco, then leaked more down his chin and onto his boots.

"Good morning, Roscoe. I was a little worried about these mares."

"What's to worry about? You're feedin' 'em about twice as much of my hay as you should."

"These big horses need more hay than smaller ones. Just like big men need more to eat that small men."

"The Rocking J has some horses that you'll want to see. Mr. Justin has imported one of the handsomest stallions I ever laid eyes upon."

"Are they Thoroughbreds?"

"Nope, but they can run a lick." Conklin spat again, then said, "That man takes horse racin' serious."

"Does Mr. Justin own the horses, or does his father?"

"Bob owns 'em. His father got kicked by one of the stallions last year. Hit him square in the face and he ain't been right in the head ever since."

"I'm sorry to hear that," Dixie said, meaning it. "Do they still have the stallion?"

"Yeah. I'm told that Bob wanted to shoot it but the horse was too valuable so they keep it locked up in a barn and use it only for breeding."

"It sounds as if that stud needs some training."

"It needs a bullet in the brain," Roscoe opined. "I never much cared for old man Justin, but I wouldn't wish his fate on my worst enemy. They bring the old man into town to see the doc every month and he don't recognize a soul."

"Isn't there anything they can do for him?"

"Nope. The doc examines Mr. Justin. Looks into his eyes and ears, then listens to his heart. But Mr. Justin just ain't right anymore, and he used to be a real stem-winder. You couldn't put a thing over on him because he was so sharp. Bob ain't no fool, but he never compared to his old man and he gets drunk too damned often."

"At least his father is alive."

"Better off if he were dead, Missy."

Dixie did not agree, but then, she couldn't honestly say how she'd feel if her own father had suffered permanent brain damage. Wishing to change the subject, she said, "Do you want me to feed the rest of your horses?"

"Do I have to pay you?"

"Nope."

"Then sure, go ahead! You gonna clean my stalls for free, too?"

"Nope."

"Don't blame you a bit. Nothin' but work there."

"You could hire me to do it for you and take it off the feed and boarding bill."

"Can't do that, Missy. Besides, I need some of that reward money."

"Roscoe, tell me the truth. Do you really think that my brother and Marshal Gus will kill or capture that gang?"

"Yep. I've watched the marshal over the years, and he's slowed some with his heart trouble and the whiskey, but he's still an awful good man with a six-gun, and he don't know the meaning of fear. I'd ride anyplace with old Gus."

"You and everyone else in Rio Paso had the chance," Dixie reminded the man. "But the marshal said that he had no offers of help."

"Well damnation, Missy! After them six boys got shot to pieces in that box canyon, can you blame anybody for not wanting to help? Them other three deputies that Gus sent out ended up almost as bad. Ain't none of us want to be dead heroes."

Dixie placed her hands on her hips. "Bob said that he might try for the reward."

Roscoe scoffed, spewing tobacco. "Bob Justin was just tryin' to impress you with his big talk."

"I don't know why."

" 'Cause you're sort of pretty," Roscoe said, his eyes dancing with amusement. "You're half girl, half woman, and maybe that's a female's most delicious time."

"Mr. Conklin!" Dixie exclaimed, ears burning. "I think you had just better watch your manners, sir!"

"Sorry," he said, not looking sorry. "Miss Dixie, I forget that you were once a Southern belle from the once high and mighty South. Ain't much left of that now, though, and you might as well stop thinkin' that you or your namesake are still special."

"The South, Mr. Conklin, will rise again. Maybe not in my lifetime or even for fifty generations, but I expect that it will one day regain its full constitutional rights. And a Southern born and bred man will someday become president of these United States!"

"Not a chance," Roscoe said, spitting tobacco. "The wounds between North and South will never heal."

"Mr. Lincoln says he'll bind the wounds."

"Like everyone else, I want to believe that President Lincoln is a good man. But you can't pass laws that end one man's abiding hatred for another."

Dixie looked away to her horses, always a source of comfort. "I can't forget the past, Roscoe. And it really hurts when I think about what my family had, and lost because of the war."

The liveryman nodded with understanding. "My advice to you is to make new dreams. Hell, the West is plenty big enough for all of 'em!"

"You sound like Ruff," Dixie said. "And I know you're both right. But back in Tennessee, things were very different. They were softer and more refined."

"The hell with refinement! That and two bits will get you a whiskey."

"You don't understand."

"I understand plenty more than you think," Roscoe said. "I understand that there ain't never any goin' back. And those that do never like what they find. Mark my words, Missy, whatever it is you and your brother want, you'll find it in this country."

"I hope you're right. And when I look at these beautiful mountains and this valley, I do sense promise. I listen to the wind as it sweeps across the open spaces, whispering, 'Be a part of me, if you are strong enough and want me bad enough.' "

Roscoe's busy eyebrows shot up with alarm. "Do you hear voices?"

Dixie laughed. "Yes, sometimes I imagine I hear the wind talking to me."

"You better stay among folks for a while, girl. I just hope that your brother and Marshal Gus get back before I run outa money feeding your big mares. Hay ain't cheap, and the price goes up later in the fall, after the last of it is harvested."

"I'll find a pasture for my mares," Dixie promised. "But first I need to find a job."

"I wish you luck."

"Any advice on where I might start looking?"

"Not if you're bound and determined to work with horses."

"I'll take what I must."

"Then I'd just start goin' from one business to the next, except for the saloons and the gunsmith shop—oh, and the saddlery."

"I can mend harness and stitch leather."

"That's a man's work."

"Why?"

Roscoe stammered, uncharacteristically at loss for words. "Well, it just is! And you need to stop tryin' to be a damned tomboy—do whatever it is that young ladies do best. Get a dress and get outa them man's clothes."

Dixie's cheeks flamed. "What ladies do best doesn't interest me, Mr. Conklin! And as for a dress, I hate 'em!"

"Tomboy," Roscoe grumbled. "You're gonna wind up a broken-down old spinster."

"For crying out loud. I'm only fifteen!"

"Out here, women have babes at thirteen."

Dixie had heard enough. She stormed off to feed the other horses. She sure didn't like the way that Roscoe talked and acted early of a morning.

Other than Wong Woo's breakfast of egg rolls, some kind of delicious nut pastry and mint tea, the morning was pretty much a bust for Dixie. She had visited all of the business establishments in town, and none of them could offer her even part-time work. The feed store had needed someone to unload wagons, and Dixie had rashly volunteered to give that a try, but when the owner showed her a stack of hundred-pound grain sacks, she couldn't lift even one and had to agree that the job was too physical.

"Something else will probably turn up," the feed store owner had offered, looking genuinely disappointed that he could not offer her a job.

Discouraged, Dixie went back to the marshal's office and took a nap. She slept for several hours, then returned to the livery, where she curried and saddled her favorite horse, a six-year-old sorrel mare named Aria, who had the disposition of a wildcat and the heart and speed of a champion.

Old High Man nickered hopefully, but Dixie said, "You need rest more than exercise."

When Roscoe appeared, Dixie said, "I'm going to exercise this mare. I'll be back soon to ride another, in an hour or so. They haven't been under saddle much in the last few weeks."

"You're a mighty fine-lookin' pair," Roscoe said, his expression openly admiring as Dixie mounted the tall sorrel. "Pretty girl, pretty mare."

"Even if I do wear a man's pants and shirt and act like a tomboy?" Dixie asked with raised brows.

"Yep."

"Thanks."

Dixie reined Aria about and trotted up the street, attracting a lot of attention and not a few whistles. Most of the cowboys were still at work out on the ranches and would not be arriving in town until early evening, but the few that did see Dixie were vocal in their admiration for the girl and her high-spirited Thorough-bred mare.

Aria wanted to run, and once Dixie was beyond town, she let the mare breeze up the road as fast as she wanted.

As they raced swiftly along, Dixie's face split into a wide grin and she was filled with exhilaration.

"Yes!" she shouted into the wind. Aria's speed was so remarkable that the wind made Dixie's eyes tear. Her worries all disappeared as she focused on her galloping horse, riding low and forward as she'd been taught by her father and brothers. Could there be anything finer than riding a fast horse on a clear, cool day?

On and on Aria ran, the horse enjoying herself as much as its rider. Ears back, neck stretched out, Aria's long legs were a blur as they devoured distance. At a mile and a quarter, Dixie slowed the mare first into an easy canter, then a trot and finally a walk. Aria wasn't breathing hard despite the altitude, and that proved to Dixie that the mare was in excellent condition.

"You're as smooth on the fly as a billiard ball rolling on felt," she said, patting Aria's neck and deciding to travel up the road another mile or two and see a little more of this beautiful valley.

Dixie lost track of time and rode longer than she'd intended. The country was so green and pretty that she was reluctant to turn around, but she really did need to exercise at least one more mare before dark, and the afternoon was already well along.

But just as she was about to turn back toward Rio Paso, Dixie heard yelps and wild whoops. She twisted around in her saddle and saw a gang of cowboys closing in on her backtrail on their way to a big night in town. Dixie trotted Aria to the side of the road so the cowboys could pass. But they had no intention of passing. They were young and brash, wearing their best shirts and pants, and when they saw Dixie, they reined up sharply and doffed their big Stetsons.

"Good afternoon, miss!" called a freckle-faced young one. "My name is Billy, and it is a real honor to make your acquaintance."

Before Dixie could answer, another grinning cowboy made the full line of introductions. "My name is Renfro Bennington. I hail from Texas. And these are my other side-kicks, Art, Moses, Pete, Dusty, Hammer, Jerome, Oliver, Bison, and Slats."

Dixie nodded and introduced herself, and each cowboy nodded back to her.

Dusty was the horse-faced, homely one, but that didn't mean he was shy. "That is one fine-lookin' mare you're ridin', Miss Ballou. Bet she can run a little, huh?"

"She can."

"Maybe you'd like to race us on into Rio Paso," Bison, the short, blocky one, suggested.

"I think not," Dixie said, for she understood the nature of the request. These young cowboys knew full well that Dixie was a Southerner, for they could hear the soft Tennessee drawl in her voice. They also could see that she wasn't riding any ordinary cow pony, and they wanted to know exactly how fast her horse was so they could judge it against their best.

"Wouldn't want to see you get hurt, or anything," Art said. "We're just talking about a nice, easy gallop into town."

"I've already given this mare her run. But thanks for the offer."

"We'd be happy to escort you into Rio Paso, miss."

"I'll be fine. You gentlemen go ahead and enjoy your-selves."

"I'd enjoy myself a whole lot more if you'd have dinner with me," Moses said, glancing out of the corners of his eyes to see the reaction of his friends to this bold invitation. "I know where they serve the best steaks in town."

"Maybe she'd rather go with me," Hammer offered, lifting straighter in his saddle. "I'm from the South."

"What part?"

"Texas," Hammer said, and quickly added, "East Texas, that is."

"She could eat with all of us," Dusty said, glowering at his companions.

"Well, I asked her first!" Moses complained.

Dixie could see that there was the potential here of a big argument that might even lead to a fight. "I thank you all," she said quickly, "but I've already made plans for dinner."

"Oh," Moses said, looking crestfallen. "Well, what about breakfast?"

"I'm afraid that I can't," Dixie said firmly. "But I appreciate your offer. Who do you work for?"

"The Justin family," Art rushed to explain. "Their spread is called the Rocking J Ranch, and it's just up the road about a mile and then off to your right into the hills. Mr. Justin has some tall racing horses like you're riding. You might want to go take a look. If so, I'll be happy to ride back with you."

"Maybe some other time."

When Dixie said no more, the cowboys took the hint. They reluctantly excused themselves like gentlemen and galloped on toward Rio Paso. As they vanished around a bend in the road, Dixie could hear the faint echoes of their joyful whoops.

Now that she was alone again, Dixie realized that she had been a little uncomfortable being surrounded by the young and ardent cowboys. Maybe, she decided, that was just part of growing up.

TEN

When Dixie returned to town, the Rocking J cowboys had tied their ponies in front of the Bulldog Saloon, and she could hear their laughter all the way out into the street. One of the cowboys happened to see Dixie through the doorway. He let out a whoop and rushed outside waving a bottle of whiskey.

With a big grin, he shouted loudly enough for everyone in Rio Paso to hear his voice, "May I have the extreme honor of buying you a drink, Miss Ballou!"

"No, thank you," Dixie called over her shoulder as the others stampeded out to join their friend.

"Sure is a pretty mare," another cowboy yelled.

"Pretty filly, too!" another hollered as they all began to hoot with laughter.

Dixie's cheeks were as red as ripe apples. When she arrived back at the livery, Roscoe looked up from a chair where he had been dozing and said, "You look a little flushed from the sun, Miss Ballou."

"I'm fine," Dixie said, unsaddling Aria and leading her back to the corral, where Dixie selected another mare for a quick exercise session.

"You going out again?"

"I am."

Roscoe shielded his eyes from the diving sun. "Ain't more'n an hour left of daylight."

"That's all the time I need."

"Suit yourself."

Dixie quickly saddled a mare she'd named Rose because she was a red roan. Rose was a handsome animal, though not as stylish or delicate as Aria. Her head was just a shade too large, her bones a trifle too heavy, her muscles too pronounced, and her conformation was not quite as perfect as some of the other Thoroughbred mares they'd trapped a few months earlier. Mares that had once been stolen by a famous outlaw stallion named Blue Bullet and then recaptured by Ruff, Dixie, and an Indian named Johnny Starving Bear.

"Ruff says we're a lot alike," Dixie explained to Rose as she checked her cinch. "Stubborn."

Rose dipped her head and stamped her feet with anticipation. Dixie finished saddling and bridling the mare and prepared to mount. Rose began to move, and Dixie yanked sharply on her reins. Rose tossed her head nervously and began to whirl.

"Hold still!"

Rose was excited, but by exercising patience, Dixie was able to calm the mare and insert her boot into the stirrup. However, each time she lifted her weight, Rose would start forward and Dixie would pull her up short, until the mare was finally forced to stand perfectly still. Only then did Dixie throw her right leg over the cantle of her saddle. She did not let the nervous animal jump forward but forced Rose to remain in place.

"Easy," she crooned. "Just settle down."

Easing up on the reins, Dixie allowed Rose to move forward. The mare tossed her head in a token gesture of defiance that caused Dixie to smile with understanding because, sometimes, even a horse needed to save a little face.

"You're astraddle a building tornado," Roscoe said with more than a little concern on his weathered face. "That red mare has a mighty short fuse."

"She needs a lot more riding than we've been giving her," Dixie explained, her attention coming to focus on Rose as they started ahead. Rose felt like a coiled steel spring.

Dixie was just opposite the Bulldog Saloon when the same bunch of Rocking J cowboys spied her again and came pouring outside shouting and yelling. Dixie knew they weren't trying to make trouble, but Rose didn't. The mare snorted, jammed her head down between her knees, and began bucking.

Nothing could have delighted the cowboys more than to see a pretty girl on a wildly bucking horse. "Hi-yah!" they bellowed, whipping off their hats to send them sailing through the air.

The mare went crazy. Rose bucked so hard that Dixie was almost thrown, and would have been if she hadn't managed to grab her saddle horn and jam her foot back into an empty stirrup. Dixie could hear the Rocking J cowboys bellowing and shouting encouragement as Rose sunfished, swapping one end with the other. Dixie slammed her heels into Rose's flanks. Rose landed stiff-legged and flat-footed on all fours. Dixie's head whipped forward, and her spine felt as if it were being driven against rock. Pain shot up and down her backbone and radiated out through her arms. Dixie's eyes momentarily lost their focus, and she held on only by instinct as Rose put on a show that brought a huge crowd rushing outside to watch. When Rose sunfished again, Dixie lost her seat and would have been hurled aside, but Rose swapped ends and came back under her. A moment later, Dixie's vision cleared and she began to fight the powerful roan. Dixie knew that the outcome of this battle might ultimately determine if the mare turned outlaw.

A vision of Ruff passed across Dixie's eyes, and she could almost hear him exhorting her to ride this mare to a standstill. He was yelling instructions at her to punish Rose just as the crazed mare was punishing Dixie with her terrible bucking. Dixie gritted her teeth and fought the roan.

Things were happening so fast that Dixie could not keep track of where she was or even what was transpiring. In the demented fury of her bucking, Rose slammed into the side of a wagon, and Dixie's leg would have been ripped off if she had not kicked her right boot out of its stirrup at the very last instant before the collision.

Rose staggered back onto her haunches and then launched herself skyward, front hooves clawing as if she were determined to scale the distant mountaintops. Three powerful jumps later, horse and rider landed across a water trough and Dixie heard the cowboys howl with appreciation as the trough collapsed like an empty eggshell and flooded the street. This caused some fool to draw his six-gun and fire it into the sky as if this were the grand finale of an Independence Day celebration.

"Dammit!" Dixie swore, her anger directed more at the cowboys than at the roan.

Rose kept bucking and squealing. The powerful animal launched herself six feet into the air and landed on the tongue of a wagon. The tongue snapped like a twig, and it was a miracle that Rose wasn't skewered. Seconds passed like hours. Dixie felt as if she were weakening, and her head began to snap back and forth. She could taste blood. Maybe she'd bitten off her tongue, but there was no time to find out. She was beginning to lose her strength and timing.

"Drag her head up, Miss Ballou!" a cowboy yelled. "Yank her head up!"

Dixie heard and knew it was exactly what Ruff would have been shouting. A horse cannot buck with its head up in the air. But the saying and the doing were two entirely different matters. Dixie strained until her arms felt as if they were tearing out of their shoulder sockets, but Rose was so powerful that the head wasn't coming up. Dixie clung to the saddle and fought to buy time, and she wondered who would quit this insanity first—her or Rose.

At least she was putting on a good show, because it sounded as if the crowd was multiplying, and over the pounding of blood in her ears, Dixie could hear people roaring with appreciation. She was almost thrown when the mare bucked into a pair of saddle horses tied to a hitching rail. Both horses snapped their reins and jumped halfway over the hitchrail trying to escape.

But Rose was finally tiring, and Dixie was able to haul up the mare's head and force her into a series of crow hops that terminated when Dixie booted the roan into a hard run. They went flying down the street, leaving a small section of Rio Paso demolished.

Dixie leaned over the mare's powerful shoulders and forced the gasping Thoroughbred on and on until they were two miles out of town and the roan's stride began to falter and her breathing turned ragged.

Dixie finally allowed the mare to slow down as sunset began to engulf the land. Brilliant tongues of fire licked the mountaintops and cast a bloodred glaze across the lazy Rio Grande. A cool breeze sprang up and made the leaves chatter as they danced against the rainbow sky.

"Have you had enough of this foolishness?" Dixie asked, allowing Rose to settle into a hard trot and then finally a walk.

Rose called it quits. The mare stopped dead in her tracks, lowered her head, and dripped sweat into the dust. Dixie dismounted and placed her hand on the exhausted animal's muzzle. "Those cowboys ought to have known better than to come storming outside and to spook you that way with their damned hats. But you had no right to throw such a tizzy, Rose. One or both of us could have gotten killed."

In answer, the mare sighed and quivered with exhaustion.

"I'm going to ride you at least an hour every day until Ruff comes back," Dixie vowed. "And by then, maybe we'll become friends."

Rose nickered weakly, and Dixie gathered her reins and punched a toe into her stirrup. She grabbed the saddle horn and lifted her weight off the ground, waiting. Rose didn't even twitch, and so Dixie threw her leg on over the cantle, gathered up her reins, and turned the horse around.

Dixie spat blood. She'd bit her tongue and it hurt like crazy. Her back also radiated pain, from her toes to her fingertips. But she was going to be all right, and Dixie knew that her late father and her brothers would have been very proud of her successful ride. Dixie had erred by allowing Rose to drop her head, but redeemed herself by proving to the animal that bucking was futile. Since early childhood, Dixie had been taught that the worst thing possible was to let a green horse like Rose buck you off. That only reinforced the idea in the animal's thinking that it could succeed as a bucker, a very, very bad habit.

"I hope you got that notion out of your mind," Dixie said. "If you haven't, we'll just have to girl it another twirl, but next time, I'll have to use a quirt."

Rose's ears twitched back and forth as she plodded back toward Rio Paso, and Dixie didn't think the mare would try to test her again—at least, she sure hoped not.

It was a beautiful evening, with one of those lingering sunsets that were peculiar to the high country of New Mexico and Colorado.

"Come on Rose," Dixie said, forcing the roan into an easy jog. "It'll be long after dark before we get back to Rio Paso, and then heaven only knows how much damage we're going to be held accountable for. I recall a busted water trough and wagon tongue, but there may be other things that I missed."

Rose didn't care. She was so weary that her gait was a shambling trot. The mare's ears were tilted slightly down, and she looked so defeated and depressed that Dixie decided to give Rose an extra bit of love and attention before unsaddling her and turning her back into the corral.

But those plans were altered when Dixie rounded a bend and saw a waiting crowd.

"Hip, hip, hooray!" someone shouted, and they all took up the call.

Rose snorted and tried to look worried, but she just didn't have the strength to put on much of a bluff.

"Hip, hip, hooray!"

Dixie wished she could have turned around and ridden off. The last thing she wanted or needed was this kind of greeting. But since it would have been ridiculous to ride off into the night, Dixie had little choice but to continue on into town.

"Where did you learn to ride like that!" a man yelled, echoing the same question that was on everyone's lips.

The cowboys were especially flattering. Dixie received no less than ten marriage proposals, and everyone wanted to buy her a drink.

"No, thank you," she kept saying as she urged the weary roan toward Roscoe's livery. "No, thank you."

Only one man was unhappy. "It's going to cost you twenty dollars to replace my wagon's busted tongue, young lady! You've no right to ride a horse you can't control."

Before Dixie could form a reply, one of the Rocking J cowboys yelled, "Come, boys, let's take up a collection for Miss Ballou! Watching that ride was worth a week's pay!"

Apparently almost everyone agreed, because a hat went around fast, and when it was brimming with money, the cowboy waltzed up to Dixie with a smile, bowed, and said, "I'm Renfro Bennington, in case you forgot."

"Are you the one that fired his gun when I was getting my brains battered into mush?"

Renfro shook his head, looking very contrite. "No, ma'am!"

Dixie supposed she should have been angry, but with that hat full of money and with the way that the Rocking J cowboys and all the others were smiling, she just couldn't muster up so much as a frown.

"Well, thank you," she said, counting out twenty dollars and giving it to the wagon's owner. "And I'm glad that you all enjoyed the show we put on, though I hope that it's not soon to be repeated."

"Miss Ballou?"

Dixie's eyes came to rest on a well-fed gentleman wearing a bowler, suit, and tie. "Yes, sir?"

"My name is Oliver T. Gates, and I've a couple of saddle horses that have, frankly, developed some real nasty habits."

"Such as?"

The man looked around, suddenly appearing embarrassed. "Well, to be honest, they kick, bite, and buck."

"Mr. Gates, that's because you and the missus ain't ridden them for six years!" a cowboy howled, while the others burst into guffaws.

"Horses do need regular exercise or they'll sour," Dixie said to the well-dressed man. "Mr. Gates, I'd be happy to take the kinks out of your horses so that you and your wife can ride in comfort and safety."

"That would be very much appreciated," the man said. "Clyde and Cindy have become pets, and my wife can't bear to sell them, and I'd like to ride them."

"And you will," Dixie promised over the laughter. "Can I start working with them tomorrow morning?"

"You bet you can, young lady. The sooner the better."

"Thank you!"

Dixie was surrounded by a crowd of admirers as she unsaddled Rose and turned the sweaty mare back into the corral. She wasn't allowed to carry her saddle into the tack room or even lift a pitchfork as cowboys and city fellas alike anticipated her every move. Dixie was offered several more jobs breaking or exercising difficult horses, and everyone kept inviting her to dinner.

"Thanks, but no thanks," she said, wanting nothing more than to eat a plate of Wong Woo's Chinese and then to stretch out on the marshal's little bunk and sleep.

Dixie's neck ached with pain, and she felt as if she had been beaten with a board. But she felt good, too. And maybe she would sample a little of Marshal Gus's whiskey. Not a lot, but enough to ease her into the sweet and deadening mercy of sleep.

ELEVEN

Dixie awoke in the night to a flurry of gunfire. She sat bolt upright on the marshal's bunk and heard a horse racing down the street followed by at least a half dozen more rapid gunshots. And then she heard a scream.

Dixie tried to shake the sleep from her eyes. She had been dead to the world, and it wasn't until someone began to pound on her door that she really came fully awake.

"Who is it!"

"Two outlaws have been shot!" a panicky voice answered.

"Then get the doctor!"

"But they're already dead."

"Then get the mortician!"

"But two more have been wounded. We need to put 'em in jail."

"Oh, dammit!" Dixie swore. "All right, just hang on while I get dressed."

The man outside muttered something that Dixie did not appreciate. Dixie had been sleeping almost fully dressed, so it didn't take but a moment to prepare herself. She fumbled for a match and lit her bedside lamp, then knuckled sleep from her eyes and pulled on her boots.

She opened the door and came face-to-face with not one, but three men. Before she could stop or even question them, they rushed inside.

"Hey!" Dixie protested. "What the devil do you think you are doing?"

The short, bearded one with the bent nose said, "Four

outlaws broke into the mayor's general store a few minutes ago. Someone heard them rummaging around inside, and when the thieves came out with their arms full of guns, rifles, ammunition, and supplies, we were armed and waitin'."

"Did you order them to surrender?"

"Nope. Mr. Justin said that enough innocent townsfolk had died in Rio Paso, and it was time we sent a message to anyone else who might decide to rob our stores or banks. So we opened fire, and all hell broke loose."

"That's right," another man said, still clutching a gun. "We killed two of 'em before they got out the door. The other two were wounded inside the store and surrendered right away. As soon as the doc has a chance to see if they're going to make it, we're locking them in this jail."

Dixie knew better than to object. If the townspeople had apprehended two thieves after a bloody shoot-out, the jail was the obvious place to contain them. But this sure did complicate her temporary living arrangements.

"Here they come!" one of the men said, whirling at the sound of heavy footsteps on the boardwalk.

The first one in the door was Bob Justin, and he wasted no time in letting everyone know exactly who was in charge. "Bring those damned thieves inside, boys! Where are the keys to the jail cell, Miss Ballou?"

Dixie stared at two badly wounded men being half carried and half dragged by an angry crowd.

"Miss Ballou, we need the keys!"

Dixie tore her eyes away from the wounded prisoners and jumped to the marshal's desk. She scooped up the key to the jail cell and quickly got it opened. The prisoners were tossed unceremoniously upon the rock floor of the cell.

The town doctor rushed inside. "Dammit, step aside and

let me through! Those men are wounded, and they'll bleed to death for certain if I don't attend to them."

"Too gawddamn bad," the owner of the saddlery hissed. "They should have known better than to come to Rio Paso after what we did to them bank robbers earlier this week."

Dixie had an urge to tell the fool that she and Ruff were the ones who'd made the bank robbers pay a price, not the townspeople. But that seemed a trivial issue right now as the doctor pushed his way into the cell, opened his medical kit, and began to try and stanch the bleeding of one of the wounded thieves.

After several moments of pressing a wad of bandaging hard against the wounded outlaw's shoulder, the doctor looked up at the excited crowd and said, "I could use someone to hold a bandage down tight so we could get this man's bleeding stopped while I work on the other man."

When no one offered to help, Dixie stepped forward, but Justin tried to drag her back. "You don't need to help him, Miss Ballou. In fact, this is no place for a lady."

"I'm not a lady," Dixie said angrily as she shook her arm free and knelt beside the doctor. "And I don't care what these men did, we can't stand by and let them bleed to death."

"Exactly," the doctor snapped, taking Dixie's hand and pressing it down hard over the bleeding shoulder wound. "Thank you, Miss Ballou."

"You're welcome."

The doctor's name was Ryder. Benjamin Ryder. Dixie had heard he was exceptionally good for what you would expect to find in a town as small as Rio Paso. Most frontier doctors were not really doctors at all. They were simply men who had a calling for medicine and healing. Maybe, early in their careers, they had been the only ones with the stomach to yank teeth and then had progressed to removing an occasional bullet or splinting a broken arm. Such men might, over the years, also be called upon to suture wounds and even deliver babies.

But as she watched Benjamin Ryder, Dixie could see that the slight, middle-aged man was very skilled and obviously possessed a formal medical education. Ryder had several of the townspeople hold the outlaw down. Using a forceps, he wasted no time or sympathy as he removed a bullet from the second man's leg.

"Forty-five caliber," Ryder commented, pitching the misshapen lead mass into the crowd of gawkers.

He cleansed the wound before applying a tight bandage to keep the bullet hole clean. Dixie guessed that the entire operation, if you could call removing a bullet an operation, was accomplished in less than ten minutes.

"Now," the doctor said, ignoring the hard looks of the townsmen who had crowded into the jail, "let me take a better look at this young man's shoulder."

"Why?" someone asked. "He's going to swing from a rope inside a week."

Ryder offered the men a withering glare. "I'm a doctor, not a judge and jury. You men had a right to protect your property and your town, but that right has ended and I've an obligation to try and save this boy's life."

Dr. Ryder cut the man's shirt off without bothering with buttons. The wounded outlaw was as pale as snow, and Dixie judged him to be only a few years older than her and certainly still in his teens.

"Is it bad, Doc?"

"Hell yes, it's bad," Ryder said calling for water and a basin so he could wash away blood and clearly see what a mess the bullet had made of the shoulder. "This looks like it was torn apart by a buffalo rifle."

"Hank Pepper shot the kid," a man proudly explained. "Old Hank always was a deadeye shot, but I reckon he missed the heart by about three inches."

"It's just my awful luck to get shot in my right shoulder," the kid said through gritted teeth. "Doc, will I be able to use it? My arm feels dead!"

"Try and wiggle your fingers."

The kid wiggled them, and Dixie expelled an involuntary breath of relief.

"He don't need no shoulder to swing from a rope," Bob Justin growled.

The kid paled even more. "You fixin' to hang us just for robbin' a damned dry goods store?"

"And for trying to kill us when we caught you."

"I didn't try and kill nobody! I was just trying to get some food. We were hungry."

"Wasn't food that you were carrying out," Justin spat, his breath reeking of alcohol. "You were stealing guns and ammunition."

"Not me. Honest!"

"Shut up or I'll kick your damn head off!" Justin swore. "Or better yet, I'll kick you in that tore-up shoulder."

Dixie was appalled. She came to her feet and pushed in between the kid and Justin. "You leave him alone!"

Justin's eyes widened. "You're taking the part of a thief?"

"It's not right for you to threaten him. Can't you see he's already suffering?"

"Well, we can take care of that little problem," Justin said with a cold smile as his followers nervously cackled.

The doctor jumped to his feet. "If you touch either one

of these men, I'll press charges against you and anyone else who gets into this. I mean it!"

Justin backed off, but he was angry. It showed in the way his lips formed a tight, bloodless line. "Doc, these two are gonna swing, and the thing to do right now is to get a couple of ropes and save some of the taxpayers' hard-earned money."

"You can't do that!" Dixie exclaimed.

"She's right," the doctor said. "If Marshal Gus were here, he'd run you all out of this office and send word tomorrow morning by telegraph that we need a circuit judge."

"The marshal isn't in charge now," Bob said.

"Well, neither are you, Mr. Justin!" the doctor bellowed.

Dixie accepted a bucket of water, probably dipped out of the horse trough. Taking the cell keys, she pulled the door closed, leaving her, the doctor, and the two wounded outlaws inside but everyone else outside.

"What the hell do you think you're doing!" Justin demanded.

"We're going to help these men survive to face trial," Dixie said. "Now, you men have saved the town, so why don't you go celebrate like good boys."

Justin's eyes tightened at the corners, but he spun on his heel and marched outside yelling, "Come along because I'm buying the drinks!"

"But what if them two sonsabitches gets the drop on the doc and that girl and kills 'em!" a man protested.

"Then it's what they deserve," Justin said, casting a hard look at Dixie and the doctor.

They slammed the door behind them on the way out, and everyone in the cell relaxed.

The doctor took the pail of water from Dixie's hands and wet his own handkerchief. He gently washed the blood from the young man's bony torso, all the while shaking his head.

"What's wrong, Doc?" the kid asked. "Am I goin' to die?"

"Not of this wound. But I don't think you'll ever be able to use this shoulder for any heavy work. It's torn all to pieces. If you survive a hangman's noose, it's going to pain you for the rest of your life."

The other outlaw, a large, unkempt, and dissipated fellow said, "We'll hang, Mitch. There's no doubt about that."

Mitch gulped, and tears welled up in his eyes. "We shouldn't a done what we did," he said brokenly. "Hugh, damned if we shouldn't have just surrendered and taken our medicine without trying to shoot our way out the front door."

"Shut up, kid," the man with the bullet in his thigh said wearily. "It don't help none to be beatin' yourself about what we should or shouldn't a done now. It's done."

Dixie looked to the doctor. "What can you do for him?"

"If this were a big city and I were a surgeon, maybe I could dig around and pull out the bone splinters. But under these primitive circumstances, he'd lose so much blood he'd go into shock and die."

"Just dig out the slug and leave everything else alone," Mitch said. "Okay, Doc? Okay?"

"Roll over," the doctor ordered.

"Huh?"

"He said to roll over!" Hugh shouted in anger and frustration.

Mitch rolled over onto his belly, the movement causing him to cry out with pain.

"Look at that," the doctor said to Dixie. "You can see the hole caused by the exiting slug."

Dixie was appalled. She'd seen shot-up men before, but never a bigger or uglier hole in a man. Even as she watched, the doctor began to extract a few pieces of the man's splintered shoulder blade.

"The most important thing now," the doctor said, slopping more water from the pail and cleansing the wound, "is just to stop the hemorrhaging."

Dixie agreed. Mitch was losing plenty of blood, which would account for his poor color. She helped the doctor bind the wound up tightly.

"What now?" the other outlaw said. "Are they gonna get liquored up and come back with a pair of nooses?"

"I don't know," Ryder replied. "But if they do, I'll try and stop them."

"We'll *both* try and stop them," Dixie corrected.

The doctor managed a tight smile. He closed his medical kit while Dixie managed to get the cell door open.

"I sure wish you'd just leave that door unlocked," Hugh said. "That way, if they come for us, we can at least die fighting."

But Dixie locked the door, saying, "If they come with hangman's ropes, they'll be enough fighting for everyone."

The doctor nodded. He locked the front door and trod wearily over to the marshal's desk, where he slumped into the man's swivel chair. Dixie returned to her bunk.

"You might as well try to sleep," the doctor advised. "If they do come back, you'll have plenty of warning."

Dixie supposed that the doctor was right. She closed her eyes and wondered if she might actually be killed trying to protect the wounded outlaws. They would be a hard pair to die over, but Dixie knew that it was the principle, not the thieves themselves, that really counted.

TWELVE

Ruff and Gus had found the box canyon where the young fools from Rio Paso had died in an ambush, but rain had washed away any clues. The ambushers' trail led south through such rugged and rocky country that Marshal Gus's buckskin went lame.

"You worthless jughead," the marshal groused as he unsaddled and unbridled the buckskin. "I hope that a cougar jumps on your back, 'cause the only way you could defend yourself is to jar him to death."

Ruff chuckled and watched as the marshal gave the lame animal a pinch of sugar before setting him free.

"Marshal Gus, I just saw you give your horse sugar," Ruff said. "It appears to me that you don't dislike that buckskin half as much as you claim."

"Oh, I dislike him plenty," the marshal argued, saddling and bridling another horse before using a boulder to climb onto the taller animal's back. "It's just that that buckskin was so ugly I never had to worry about anyone stealing him."

"I see your point."

"Having an ugly horse or an ugly wife has its advantages," the marshal continued. "Since nobody would want them, you can leave 'em damn near anywhere."

"Was your wife ugly?"

"No, and that was part of the problem. My wife was beautiful, just like my daughters. Men would take second and third looks at my wife and I'd get mad and start to fight."

"And I'll bet you usually won."

"Never lost until I was forty and a young fella about your age and size whipped me down to a nubbin'. He was so fast with his hands I couldn't get out of the way of his punches. I'd start to think about ducking about the time his fist would collide with my ugly mug. When I charged him, he'd dance outa my way like he was floating on air. I got all winded and tired after a while, and he kept pepperin' me in the face with his fists until my eyes swelled shut, then he got serious and started throwing heavy punches to my big gut. He beat me to my knees, then he helped me back to my feet, shook my hand, and walked away."

"He sounds like he'd learned how to really box."

"Yeah," the marshal said, "I heard that he whipped a lot of men like me until one day an old boy just pulled out a derringer and shot the kid to death."

"Did the shooter hang?"

"Yep. I helped hang him myself. Buried the both of 'em in our cemetery."

"Humph," Ruff grunted, looking back at the runty buckskin and hoping the sorry-looking animal would heal and run wild, free at last of men and their cruel mockery.

Later that day, when the tracks they were following took a sudden change of direction, Gus climbed down from his horse and said, "My guess is that these boys are heading for that hellhole called Cyclone."

"Where's that?"

"It's southwest of here," Gus explained. "Cyclone is about as rough-and-ready a mining camp as you'll ever visit. They can't keep a marshal more than a few days before he's either run off or shot."

"Sounds like a hard town."

"It is," Gus agreed. "It's ruled by outlaws and some maverick miners that only work about half the time, while they raid or rustle horses and cattle the other half. I've been warned to stay out of Cyclone or I'll be shot on sight."

"So what are you going to do?"

"I haven't decided yet," Gus confessed. "I'm not up to taming the whole damn town, and you're not either. Maybe I'll send you in there to sniff around."

"But that last bank robber will recognize me."

"Don't be too sure of that. After all, the lead was flying and he really didn't have time to get a good look at you."

"I think you're wrong," Ruff argued. "And anyway, he'd certainly recognize my stallion, High Fire."

"Then ride in alone on my new horse," Gus said as if the answer was all too obvious.

"I'll think about it," Ruff replied, not very happy with this new plan. "But damned if I'm going to ride into a death trap."

"You can ride in after dark with your hat pulled down low. No one will recognize you, and they'll all be drunk. Ask some questions. Try to spot the last bank robber or learn something that will help us find him and the ones that gunned down our boys in that box canyon."

"You make it sound real easy."

"Nothing is easy," Gus said. "But does it make any sense for me to ride into Cyclone and then we both get blown out of our saddles?"

"I suppose not."

"Then we're just wastin' time and wind talking this over," Gus grumped. "Ruff, you're going to have to ride in there by yourself."

"And what will you be doing while I'm risking my neck?"

"Snoozing," the marshal said, unable to smother a smile.

"That's about what I thought," Ruff said irritably. "So how far is it to Cyclone?"

"About thirty miles as the crow flies."

"And as we ride?"

"About forty because we have to skirt a couple of cliffs and canyons."

"Then, if we push hard, we should be there by tomorrow evening," Ruff said.

The marshal dipped his chin in agreement and swiveled around in his saddle for a last look at his buckskin. "I just hope that some damned Apache don't catch up that buckskin and eat him. That's about all he's good for right now."

"You really liked that horse."

"Like hell I did!"

But Ruff knew better.

It was about nine o'clock the next evening when they arrived at the outskirts of Cyclone. Ruff and the marshal dismounted on a high shelf of land and squatted on their heels. The town was clearly visible and, judging from the number of lights that Ruff could see, was bigger than he'd expected.

"How many people live there?"

"Maybe two hundred," the marshal answered. "Enough that you can ride in and not be noticed. But not so many that you won't be able to find our killers."

Ruff scowled. "And where will you be?"

"I'll camp right here," the marshal announced. "There's a clear stream just over yonder and plenty of grass for your horse."

"If anything happens to me, I want you to return him to

Dixie," Ruff said. "You have to promise me that."

"Nothing will happen if you keep your mouth shut and your hat brim pulled down real low," Gus said. "Just have a couple of beers in the saloons and listen."

"Fair enough," Ruff said. "But seeing as how I'm risking my life and you're going to go to sleep, how about you buyin' my beers?"

"Can't," the marshal said. "Beers would not be approved as a legitimate expense by the town council."

Ruff ground his teeth in frustration. He unsaddled and unbridled High Fire, hating to leave the animal, even though he trusted Gus.

"After he's watered, I'm going to hobble him up pretty short," Ruff announced. "But you keep a close eye on him."

"Stop worrying!" Gus shouted, spreading his bedroll under the shade of a pine and stretching out with a yawn.

Ruff was worried yet saw no choice but to carry out the plan that they'd outlined. So he stowed his saddle and bedroll in the brush, took his carbine and an extra pocketful of tobacco, and started to mount Gus's horse.

"Whoa up there," the marshal said, sitting up with a grin. "I don't think it would be a good idea to carry that carbine into town."

"Why not!"

"It just sort of announces to everyone that you're loaded for bear."

"Then that's to the good," Ruff said.

"The pistol is all you'd have time to use," Gus said, trying to stifle a yawn. "Them boys in Cyclone are pretty handy with guns. If worse came to worst, you'd have to shoot fast with that six-gun, and a rifle would just be a bother."

Ruff listened but rejected the advice. He was, to be honest, getting a little tired of traveling with Marshal Gus and doing all the cooking and the taking care of the horses while Gus napped, ate, and slept. And now Ruff was the one whose life was about to be put into jeopardy, instead of the marshal's, whose job it was to administer justice.

"If you aren't back by tomorrow morning," Gus said with a wink, "I'll consider you dead."

Ruff shot him a hard look. "If that should happen, make sure Dixie gets my stallion."

"I will. And maybe I should just tell your pretty kid sister that you decided to become a miner and work a claim right here in Cyclone."

"Don't be stupid."

"I was only kidding," Marshal Gus said. "Damn you are grouchy!"

"And you are just about the laziest son of a bitch I ever had the misfortune to ride the trail with."

Gus thought that was real funny, and he was still laughing when Ruff galloped off toward the hellhole known as Cyclone.

THIRTEEN

Cyclone was indeed a very hard town. There were whores and miners staggering around drunk in the street, laughing, fighting, and cursing. Every alley and gap between buildings was littered with garbage through which hogs gleefully rooted alongside skinny dogs. A fire-gutted building was being used as a goat pen, and several of the establishments were leaning with the wind and in imminent danger of complete collapse.

Fly-bitten horses and ferret-faced men eyed Ruff suspiciously as he rode up the dim street, hat pulled down low. A fight between a whore and her pimp broke out on the upstairs balcony of a hotel. Cursing and screeching like a witch, the whore coldcocked her pimp with a bottle of whiskey, knocking him through a railing and the rickety porch below. No one even bothered to see if the unconscious man was still breathing.

"Hey, mister! You got any money?" a woman bathed in smoky lamplight called out to Ruff in a shrill voice.

Ruff turned to see a sloe-eyed blonde with a plunging neckline bend over to lift her skirts high and adjust her red lace garter. When she leered at him, Ruff blushed with embarrassment.

"No, ma'am."

"That's all right, handsome," the girl said, favoring Ruff with a dark-toothed smile. "I'll trade you that old rifle for a little fun."

Ruff did not slow the progress of his horse. "Sorry. I need the carbine."

The blonde forgot about her garter and followed him like a dog, her expression growing desperate. "You must have something you can trade for a good time."

"Sorry."

The blonde turned away with disgust. Ruff was propositioned several more times before he came to a broken-down livery and dismounted. There was a kerosene lamp hanging from a spike driven in the door. It gave off just enough light to see that the barn was listing badly. Ruff wouldn't have sent his worst enemy into that barn, with holes in its roof large enough for eagles to fly through. All considered, this was the worst livery Ruff had ever encountered, but it was the only one in town.

Since no one came out to greet him, Ruff watered the marshal's horse and tied it to a hitching post. He heard a gunshot somewhere up the street and whirled, his hand streaking for his holster. Ruff's six-gun came free in a blur, hammer back, barrel steady.

"Easy there, stranger," a voice called from the direction of a pile of straw. "There ain't no shooting yet at this end of town."

Ruff turned to see a filthy, shirtless man lying in a pile of straw. The man wore a formless hat, and his feet were bare and dirty. "Who are you?"

"In Cyclone, that's a question that can get a man killed real quick."

"I'm holding the gun," Ruff said. "Are you the man that owns this establishment?"

"This what?"

Ruff's brow knitted. "This sorry excuse for a livery."

"Yeah, I own it," the man said, taking no offense to

Ruff's less than complimentary reference. "My name is Bertram Davenport. My father, Clyde Davenport, owned it for ten years then he got hisself shot while dickering with an outlaw over the price of a wind-broke horse. Pa was only fifty-two years old, but successful enough to leave me a business."

"Glad to hear that, Bertram. Now, I want you to watch over my horse for a little while," Ruff said. "Feed him grain and then some hay."

"It's gettin' late, so why don't you just unsaddle and turn him in with the others?" the man said. "I already fed them once and won't do it again till mornin'."

"You will if you want to be paid tonight," Ruff insisted. "I want this horse kept saddled and bridled. I won't be in town very long."

Bertram looked pained. "Horses don't like to eat with a bit in their mouth, mister."

"I know."

Bertram pushed himself up to his feet, brushed the straw away, and said, "How come you're wanting to keep your horse ready to ride? You here to kill someone and then light out of Cyclone real fast?"

"No, of course not," Ruff said, looking away because the question was uncomfortably close to the mark. He saw no point in confessing to this lazy busybody that he might very well be recognized by the last bank robber and be forced to leave on the run. If that were the case, it'd be poor planning indeed if his horse wasn't ready to ride.

"Well, then I don't understand," Bertram said, actually looking confused. "Why would you come here after dark only to ride out before first light?"

"I'm looking for someone," Ruff patiently explained. "If I find him, I'll deliver a message and leave right away. If I don't find him, then I'll still leave tonight."

Bertram gave up trying to understand. "This is still gonna cost you a dollar for the feed, even if you leave before your horse eats his fill. I charge extra when it interrupts my sleep."

"That's fair," Ruff said, digging into his pockets and making a mental note to ask the marshal for reimbursement later.

"Shall I at least loosen your damned cinch?"

"Better not," Ruff decided.

"Well fer cripssakes! You sure are planning on leaving mighty sudden like. Who is this fella you come to find?"

"Beats me," Ruff said, drawing his carbine from its saddle boot and turning to walk away.

Bertram followed him a little ways. "Stranger, you're fixin' to shoot somebody. But if that fella shoots you first, I'm keepin' this horse."

Ruff kept walking. There was nothing at all that he liked about this town, and he just hoped that Bertram did not feed the marshal's horse mildewed hay and give him the colic.

Ruff decided that he might just as well start at the nearest saloon and work his way down one side of the street and back the other. He was pretty sure that he would recognize the bank robber who'd tried to kill him.

There were six saloons, three on each side of the street, and it wasn't until Ruff came to the fifth one that he noticed a group of men around a card table and thought that the big one looked to be his man. Trouble was, in the poor light and with the air fouled with smoke, Ruff just could not be sure.

Ruff ordered and nursed a beer, watching the game for a while as he tried to make sure that the man he was looking at really was the last surviving bank robber.

"Stranger, are you about ready for another beer?" the

bartender asked, leaning across a plank to regard Ruff without warmth.

"Nope."

"Well, yours is long gone."

Ruff held his glass up to the lamplight. "Yeah, it sure is."

"Are you lookin' for a card game?"

"That's right."

"Might be they'll let you sit in at that empty chair. Those are good boys and they play a real honest game."

"I'll bet."

The bartender stared hard at Ruff. "Mister, are you trying to be a wiseass?"

"Nope."

"Then either drink or play cards. This ain't no train station for folks to stand around in and gawk at my regular customers."

"I've been gawking?"

"You have."

"Who is that big fella wearing the red flannel shirt and black suspenders?"

The bartender snatched away Ruff's empty glass. "Mister, are you the law or a bounty hunter?"

"No," Ruff said, perhaps too quickly.

"Well, mister, in Cyclone, you don't ask questions unless you want the answer in lead. You savvy?"

"I do."

"Then either buy a fresh beer, or leave. You're starting to make some of my regulars nervous."

"They don't look nervous to me."

"They are," the bartender said. "I can see their trigger fingers starting to twitch."

"Then give me another beer so they can relax."

Ruff paid another two bits for a glass of green beer. Look-

ing bored, he moseyed over toward the card table. Ruff was
not a good player and had never had much interest in poker,
faro, or any of the other games of chance so popular in
saloons and on Mississippi riverboats. His late father had
been a real fine card player. In fact, Justin had used that
talent to win his first Thoroughbred stallion, High Dancer,
who became the foundation sire of the Ballou horses. But
even Justin had admitted that there were better men with a
deck of cards and that he'd gotten uncommonly lucky that
night over thirty years ago in Richmond, Virginia.

"Mind if I sit in?" he asked to no one at the table in
particular while forcing a friendly smile.

They all studied him, and Ruff met their eyes one by one,
saving the man he thought might be the bank robber for the
last. His heart was pounding wildly, and it didn't slow a
beat when he realized that his first impression had been cor-
rect and the man in the red flannel shirt was the one that had
tried to kill both him and Dixie just south of Rio Paso.

When the big man didn't register any mutual recognition,
Ruff relaxed, wondering if these other players had been part
of the crowd that had staged the Alder Creek ambush. Well,
he thought, there is only one way to find out, and that is to
sit down and play cards.

"This is a private game, kid," the big man said coldly.
"Go find yourself another game."

"This is the only game in the room."

"Find another saloon," a second man hissed. "Get lost!"

Ruff knew that it would be suicide to protest if the other
players were all together. So he ate humble pie and smiled.
"Whatever you say, boys."

He went back to the bar. "I guess they don't want to lose
their money tonight."

The bartender snorted with derision. "Them boys wouldn't

lose anything. You'd be the one that lost. They'd drill you quicker than you could snap your fingers. That big fella is named Laredo and he's killed plenty."

"And his friends?"

"Stranger, they're all quick with a gun. Just get out of here before they decide to see how much fun they can have with a pilgrim."

"Maybe I will," Ruff said, downing his beer and heading for the door. "But I'll be back."

"Bring your money," the bartender said.

Ruff left the saloon, sure that he had found the ambushers. But, somehow, he was going to have to connect Laredo with the other members of his gang of cutthroats and ambushers. For now, however, he'd pushed his luck far enough, and all he wanted to do was to return to his camp and get some sleep. He couldn't imagine what tomorrow would bring or what Marshal Gus would ask him to do next.

But one thing for sure, it would be his neck lying out on the chopping block, not the marshal's.

When Ruff returned to their camp outside of town, he had to shake the marshal out of a deep slumber. "Wake up, Gus!"

The marshal groaned and batted at Ruff's hand. Almost instantly, he began to snore.

"Dammit, wake up," Ruff said, cuffing the man across the back of his head.

Gus said something very uncomplimentary, and it was clear that he was angry, but Ruff didn't care. "One thing sure, Marshal, no one is going to sneak up on you in the dark."

"Aw, shut up! What time is it?"

"How would I know? I sold my pocket watch a long time ago."

Gus knuckled the sleep from his eyes. "Did you find 'em?"

"I think so."

"What is that supposed to mean?"

"It means that I found the bank robber. His name is Laredo and he's got a reputation."

"So do I," Gus growled. "Did you kill him?"

"Of course not! He was playing cards with some of his friends. I wouldn't have stood a chance if I'd tried to take him."

"Then what the hell are you here for? Why didn't you wait until he left and then take him down in the dark?"

Ruff sighed. "Listen, Marshal Gus, you're the law. Not me. Besides, I haven't a clue as to whether or not the other men with him were involved in that Alder Creek ambush. Seems to me that we need to find that out before we try and take Laredo."

"Hmmm," Gus mused. "You may be right."

"So what do we do?"

"Well," Gus said, stifling a yawn, "since I can't ride into Cyclone, you're just going to have to keep going back and keeping your nose to the wind and your ears to the wall. Sooner or later, you'll learn what we need to know."

Ruff shook his head. "I should have guessed that your plan involved no risk on your part and nothing but risks on my own."

"You want to earn that reward, don't you?"

"Well, sure! But it won't do me any good if I'm dead."

"I'd split it with your little sister."

"How generous of you," Ruff said, voice filled with sarcasm. "Seeing as how I'm doing everything and all you're planning to do is sleep and eat."

"Life is never very fair," Gus said. "I recall, when I was your tender age, that I often had to do the dirty work while a more experienced lawman pulled my strings like I was his own personal puppet."

Ruff hobbled the marshal's horse, grabbed up his bedroll, and went to get some sleep.

"You're just going to have to keep going back into Cyclone until you find out what we need to know."

"And when I do," Ruff said, stretching out and looking up at the stars, "will you finally help out?"

"I'll be there, rested and ready."

"The rested part I can believe," Ruff said, closing his eyes in preparation for sleep.

FOURTEEN

Dixie was awakened several times in the night by the sound of the two wounded men calling for the doctor. Each time, she went to see if she could help but was told to go back to sleep, which she did, until the sun began to streak into the marshal's office. And now it was morning.

"Doctor?"

He had been dozing in the marshal's chair, and he awoke with a start. "Yeah?"

Dixie rolled off the bunk and went over to the doctor. "You look like you've had a tough night."

"I did have," the doctor said. "The younger prisoner is in a lot of pain."

"Do you have anything that would help him?"

"Laudanum," the doctor said. "It's a derivative of opium, and I've got the kid pretty heavily sedated. His friend won't take a thing."

"I'm sorry that you couldn't get much sleep."

"The time to sleep is in your grave," the doctor said. "I'll be fine when this is over."

"Will they come again with nooses?"

"I don't think so. At least, not in broad daylight. They might get drunk and come again tonight. I just wish to God that Marshal Gus was here. He'd stop them cold."

"I wish he and my brother were both here," Dixie said.

"Hey, miss," the older prisoner named Hugh called. "Is there a hanging party gathering up outside?"

Dixie went over to the window and pulled aside the shade. She looked up and down the street and didn't see any crowd forming.

"The street looks empty."

Hugh gripped the bars and balanced on his one good leg. "I'm in an awful lot of pain, Doc. Think you could give me some of that same stuff you gave Mitch?"

"His shoulder is far worse than your leg."

"Come on, Doc! I'm suffering! Just give me a little, will ya?"

The doctor leaned forward in his office chair and then rolled onto the balls of his feet. He looked exhausted as he trudged across the marshal's office to the cell, then opened it.

"I really appreciate this, Doc."

Dixie went back to her bunk and lay down. She felt worn out and wondered how this day would end. She was hoping that last night's drunken crowd would have come to their senses by this morning.

I should go find some strong coffee for the doc and myself, she thought. Wong Woo's tea isn't going to be enough to get either of us started.

But just as Dixie was about to climb back to her feet, she heard a strangled cry from the cell. She twisted her head around, and her jaw dropped because Hugh had somehow snatched the doctor's scalpel from his medical kit and was now holding it to the physician's throat.

"What are you doing!" Dixie cried, jumping for the rifle cabinet.

"Don't move or I'll cut him from ear to ear!" the prisoner cried. "I mean it!"

Dixie froze. She could hear the wild desperation in Hugh's voice. "All right."

"Mitch, wake up! We're getting the hell out of this town."

But the kid didn't move. Dr. Ryder choked, "He's out from the laudanum. You could drop a burning ember on his chest and he wouldn't rouse."

Not believing the doctor, the thief used his good leg to propel a kick. "Come on, kid! We're getting the hell out of here before them vigilantes come back to put nooses around our necks."

But the kid didn't move.

"Put the scalpel away," Dixie pleaded. "Have you forgotten that Dr. Ryder saved your life?"

"Unless I get out of here right now, it ain't going to do me any good. The town will get liquored up again tonight and finish what they set out to do last night."

"We'll stop them again."

Hugh shook his shaggy head. He would have been a handsome enough man except that he was so dirty and unkempt and he had a knife scar running across his cheek. "Missy, you just lay down on that bunk and don't you move. The doctor and I are going to take a little stroll to the nearest horse, and then I'm gettin' outa this town. I ain't never coming back!"

"Please, just leave the doctor behind," Dixie begged. "You can move a lot faster that way."

"No! 'Cause, if they're waiting . . ."

Dixie didn't need to hear the man finish his thought. If the townspeople were waiting, they'd open fire at the sight of the escaping prisoner.

The doctor gulped, and the scalpel cut flesh. Dixie gasped when she saw blood trickle down the doctor's neck and stain his starched white collar.

"Please, just take a rifle and leave."

"Uh-uh," Hugh said, pushing the doctor ahead of him. Dr. Ryder's fear showed in his eyes, but he was also quiet, not given to begging for his life.

Hugh looked around the room. "Miss, I need a loaded six-gun and . . . and that sawed-off shotgun in the rifle rack. Yeah, that ought to do it."

Shoving the doctor forward, the thief guided him over to the rifle rack, where the outlaw grabbed the shotgun and broke it open. Satisfied that both barrels were loaded, Hugh dropped the scalpel. Cocking the hammers, he pointed the shotgun at the doctor's back. "Are you packin'?"

"Packing what?"

"A derringer or a hideout gun!"

"Of course not," Ryder said as if he'd been insulted. "I'm a physician. A healer and protector of life."

The thief turned to Dixie. "You've got a six-gun, don't you?"

"No."

"All right," he whispered, thinking out loud. "Let's just waltz out the door and we'll steal a fast horse. You stay real close, Doc. Don't try and break away or shout for help. Because, if you do, then I'll open you up like a sardine can."

"As you wish," the physician whispered. "I'm not eager to die, and I don't want to see a shoot-out. I hope you escape without firing a shot."

"Yeah, well, so do I. But remember one thing. I'd rather go down fighting than put on a show rope-dancing with the devil."

Dixie believed the man, and so, apparently, did the doctor. He went to the door and opened it a crack. "It looks clear, and I can see a couple of horses about forty yards up the street."

"Then let's get to 'em," Hugh said, hobbling forward, his eyes feverish and his lips pulled from his teeth in a grimace. "The sooner I get out of Rio Paso, the happier I'll be."

"If that leg wound breaks open on horseback, you could bleed to death," Ryder cautioned. "In fact, you probably would bleed to death."

"Still better than hanging." Hugh looked over at Dixie and said, "Thanks for helpin' us last night. You're the kid's only chance to keep his neck from getting stretched."

"I'll do whatever I can, but I think that you're making a terrible mistake."

"Well, it ain't the first," Hugh said fatalistically before he shoved the doctor outside.

The moment they were gone, Dixie grabbed her pistol, which had been concealed by blankets, and rushed to the door. Her breath caught in her throat as she watched the doctor being marched down the boardwalk with Hugh pressing close behind. The shotgun was tucked solidly in between them and was barely visible.

Maybe they'll make it, she thought.

Dixie's heart pounded so hard that she thought it might actually burst. Her breath seemed to catch in her throat, and she couldn't breathe until Hugh and the doctor finally reached the two horses. Then, she saw the doctor and Hugh untie a pair of saddled horses. Dixie realized that it made excellent sense for Hugh to steal an extra horse, but it would also attract considerable attention.

"Hurry!" Dixie whispered frantically.

Everything was going fine until the thief tried to lift his wounded leg into the stirrup. Dixie witnessed a flash of pain across Hugh's face, and she saw his mouth open in a silent scream as the wounded thief struggled to lift his boot the last few inches.

The doctor grabbed the thief's boot and actually jammed it into the stirrup. Hugh made a desperate attempt to mount the horse, but his bad leg wouldn't bear the pain. Dixie saw the leg buckle and then watched as the doctor struggled mightily to hoist Hugh up into the saddle.

Someone bellowed a warning, and that made Hugh and Dr. Ryder struggle all the harder. Ryder was not a strong man, but his adrenaline must have been pumping because he managed finally to shove Hugh into the saddle. The thief swayed and dropped his reins.

"The prisoner is escaping! Shoot him!" someone yelled as men poured out of the saloons and storefronts, drawing their guns.

Hugh panicked. Unable to reach his reins, he made a desperate grab for the horse's bridle and then tried to drag the horse's head around and boot it into a run. But the animal stampeded ahead in fear and tried to jump the hitchrail. Hugh lost his balance, and the shotgun tumbled from his hands as bullets screamed in from every direction.

"Dr. Ryder, get down!" Dixie cried.

Ryder, exhausted and confused because of a night without sleep, cast his eyes about as if trying to decide where to run. He took a bullet in the head and fell as if he'd been poleaxed. Dixie began to run as more bullets riddled Hugh, twisting him this way and that in the saddle. He rolled off the horse, but his boot caught in the stirrup. The terrified animal wheeled away and dragged the dead man for nearly fifty feet before Hugh's boot tore free and his body came to a rest.

Dixie ran to the doctor's side, but the poor man was dead. A bullet had passed through his right ear and exited just above his left eye. He probably hadn't felt a thing and had died instantly.

Dixie wept. This had been a very good man and a wonderful doctor, and now—his life, his gift, his talent, all wasted.

"Jezus," someone muttered, "I wonder which one of us killed poor Doc Ryder."

Dixie looked up, wiping her eyes dry. "You all killed him!"

"But it was an accident!"

"It was stupidity!" Dixie cried, her eyes hot with anger. "Exactly how far do you think our prisoner could have ridden with a bullet hole in his leg? Why, you would have found him not more than a mile from this town. Instead, you had to shoot him to pieces! And in doing that, you also killed your doctor!"

Dixie climbed to her feet. "I'm going back to the marshal's office. If any of you try and take my other prisoner, you'd better come in shooting."

None of them said a word, and when Dixie's eyes landed on Bob Justin, he looked away, his unshaven face slack with shame and dissipation.

Dixie trudged back to the marshal's office, thinking about Ruff and wishing to God that he were here to help make things right.

Mitch was still asleep in the cell, and Dixie locked the front door and collapsed on the marshal's bunk. She could not believe the waste of such a valuable life. Dr. Ryder was the kind of man you could never replace on this Western frontier.

When Mitch woke up a few hours later and realized that he and Dixie were alone, he said, "Where's Hugh and that doctor?"

"It's a long story and not a good one."

Mitch sat up fast. "Has something happened to them?"

"Your friend tried to escape."

"Not without me he wouldn't."

"You were too drugged to wake up. Hugh decided to go alone. While trying to steal a horse, he and the doc were shot to death on the street."

Mitch covered his face. "I'm dead," he whispered. "I ain't got a chance of getting out of this alive."

"Yes, you do."

Mitch's hands dropped, and he choked. "Miss Ballou, we both know they'll be coming for me tonight."

"I don't know any such thing."

"But they will!"

Dixie didn't know if that was true or not. All she knew for sure was that trouble had dogged her every movement since she and Ruff had first entered this accursed Rio Grande Valley.

"Mitch, have you ever been to Denver?"

He took a moment to compose himself. "Sure. I worked at the Denver stockyards for about six months."

"Did you like the town?"

"Yeah, but it's pretty big." Mitch perked up a little. "How come you're asking about Denver?"

"Me and my brother are fixing to go live there. Maybe we'll develop a Thoroughbred horse ranch in that area."

"You'd want to buy flat land out on the eastern edge of town," Mitch advised, acting glad to push away his own dark thoughts. "There's some real nice little ranches, but mostly it's farms."

"We'd need only a hundred acres or so," Dixie explained. "Later on, we could buy more property."

"Land runs about a dollar an acre in that country. But the earth is rich, plenty fit for a plow. I'd raise wheat out there. If a man had a little stake, he could earn his living off a section of that eastern Colorado prairie."

"You come from a farm family?"

"Yep," Mitch said. "But I guess you find that hard to believe, seeing me now."

"You don't look like a farmer."

"That's because I never wanted to look like a farmer. Bib overalls and big, clunky, round-toed shoes. No, ma'am! Followin' a plow up and down a field is not my idea of exciting."

A dark cloud passed across Dixie's eyes. "I just wish it hadn't gotten so exciting out there on the street. This town won't ever be able to replace Dr. Ryder."

"How'd the doc get drilled?"

"He forgot to duck his head."

"I'm real sorry about that, miss. He was a fine doctor, and he probably saved my life."

"I'm sure that he did."

Mitch gulped. "But all for nothing."

Dixie could not meet the young man's eyes. "Probably," she said, wondering how she was going to make sure that Mitch received the benefit of a fair trial instead of getting lynched.

"Miss Ballou?"

"Yes?"

"Do you suppose you could give me some more of that painkiller?"

"I think that you'd better wait until the pain gets worse," Dixie advised. "Because there might not be much left."

"There's always whiskey, but that never brought me nothing but grief."

Dixie sat down on her bunk and then stretched out full, with her pistol resting easy in her hand.

"What are you going to do when those vigilantes come for me tonight?" Mitch asked.

"I don't know."

"Ain't no sense in your dying, too," Mitch said after a long silence. "I almost wish they'd a hanged us last night. If they had, the doctor would still be alive and I wouldn't be worried sick right now."

"I hadn't thought of it that way."

"Well, I'm right, ain't I?"

Dixie didn't have an answer as she studied Mitch's anxious face. He was young and still boyish. His hair was a sandy brown, and he had dimples in his cheeks and nice, honest-looking eyes.

"I sure wish you hadn't tried to rob the general store," Dixie said. "It was a real bad mistake."

"I didn't want to. They got me to drinkin' and I finally said yes."

"If you get out of this mess alive," Dixie told him, "you ought to swear off drinking anything stronger than coffee."

"I sure will do that, miss! Yes, I will!"

Dixie rolled her head back and stared up at a fly-specked ceiling. Her eyelids were heavy, and she drifted off thinking of better days and of her brother, Ruff. My oh my, how she wished that he were here.

FIFTEEN

Dixie would never forget that day because, shortly after noon, a rider came pounding into Rio Paso shouting something and waving a newspaper.

"There's something going on," Dixie said, looking out the window and seeing people gathering in the street. Many of those she saw, on hearing the news, buried their faces in their hands and wept.

Dixie could not figure this out. "I've got to find out what's wrong."

"You're going to leave me here alone!"

"I'll just step outside," Dixie promised. "I won't let anyone between myself and the door."

"I wish you wouldn't!" Mitch came to his feet, face very anxious. "Please don't open that door!"

But Dixie had already made up her mind. She had never witnessed such a sorrowful scene as the one that was taking place on the street. People were milling about looking, well, almost dazed. Most of the women were in tears, and some of the men were openly sobbing.

"There must have been some terrible calamity or disaster," Dixie said, unbolting the door.

"There's going to be one right here if you let them get the drop on you, miss!"

But Dixie had no intention of letting anyone get the drop on her. She stepped outside with a rifle cradled in her arms and her pistol stuffed into her belt.

"What's going on!" she called to a woman nearby who

was weeping and hugging a small girl. "What's wrong? Did more people get shot?"

"No," the woman said, looking up with her eyes already red and swollen. "We've just learned that President Lincoln has been assassinated."

"What!"

"Someone shot him dead at a theater."

Dixie leaned the rifle against the front of the marshal's office and sank down to draw her knees up to her chin. As a Southerner, she had not been overly fond of Lincoln, but she'd admired him and believed those who said that Lincoln possessed an innate fairness that would go a long way to healing the wounds between the North and the South. But now Lincoln was dead.

"I'm sorry," Dixie said, genuinely meaning it. "Do you know anything about the vice president?"

"Not a thing. But there will never be another man like President Abraham Lincoln. He freed the slaves and he released the Confederate prisoners at—"

"He released them?" Dixie's immediate thought was of her missing brother, Houston.

"Almost a month ago," the woman said. "But God only knows what is going to become of this nation without our beloved President Lincoln."

Hope stirred in Dixie's breast. If Lincoln freed the prisoners, she thought, maybe my brother Houston will be coming to find me and Ruff!

"Are you smiling?" the woman asked, peering closely at Dixie. "Dear God, are you daft!"

"No, ma'am, I'm not daft, and I am grieved to hear about Mr. Lincoln being shot."

"You certainly don't sound as if you are grieving!"

Dixie ducked back into the marshal's office and rebolted

the door. She placed the rifle back in its rack and sat down on her bunk.

"Well," Mitch asked. "What's wrong?"

"President Lincoln was assassinated."

Mitch was silent for a moment. "That's what all the fuss is about?"

"Yes."

"Hell," Mitch groused, going back to his bunk. "Lincoln didn't do nothing for the folks out here. Ain't no big thing to me that he's dead."

"There are a lot of people out in the street who feel differently," Dixie told her prisoner. "The president was supposed to be a great man."

"He didn't do nothing for the Western farmers or ranchers," Mitch said. "And he sure wouldn't have done nothing to save my neck from getting stretched."

Dixie was hardly listening. She was thinking about Houston Ballou, her oldest surviving—possibly surviving—brother. Houston had gone north to find his love, a Southern belle named Molly O'Day who had been spying for the South and had been operating in Washington. That had been, oh, more than a year ago.

Was Houston still alive? Was Ruff still alive? Dixie didn't know. All she was certain of was that if both of her brothers were still alive, then they had a family and a chance at rebuilding their father's prize Thoroughbred bloodline.

"Miss?"

Dixie's head snapped up as she was pulled from her thoughts. "Yes?"

"You're smiling," Mitch said. "Didn't you like the president?"

"My loyalties were with the South and President Jefferson

Davis," Dixie explained. "Like many Southerners, I despised generals Sherman and Grant, but not Mr. Lincoln."

"None of that war stuff matters to me anymore. Not when I know that I'm probably going to dance at the end of a rope tonight."

But Dixie shook her head. "I don't think so."

"Why not?" Mitch demanded, coming to his feet.

"Because I think the people of Rio Paso have had their fill of death."

Mitch didn't understand. You could see that he did not by the confused look on his grimy young face. Dixie, however, did not much care if Mitch understood or not. What was important was that if Houston had been languishing in a Northern prison all this time, he might be on his way south, and then he'd follow their trail, and somehow, Dixie was sure, he would rejoin them very soon.

That evening, Mayor Morton and two more somber gentlemen came to pay a visit. They filed into the marshal's office and stood rather awkwardly near the front door.

Dixie trusted the mayor, but she didn't know a thing about the other two men so she kept her gun close at hand.

"Miss Ballou, this is Mr. Oakes and Mr. Taylor. They are friends and members of our town council."

Dixie nodded to them, then looked back to the mayor, who said, "We're here to say that we think it is best for everyone if the prisoner is taken to Santa Fe for a trial. He'd be hanged for sure if he stands trial in our town."

"It's a trick!" Mitch cried. "They just want to get me out of this jail and then kill me out on the road somewheres."

"It's no 'trick,' young man. Today is one of the blackest days in the history of Rio Paso. We loved Dr. Ryder. The town is devastated by his loss. And now, as if we didn't have enough to grieve over, there's the assassination of President Lincoln. We just want you out of town—the sooner the better."

"Who's going to take him?" Dixie wanted to know.

"We've wired Santa Fe for help. Their sheriff is sending his best deputy, a fella named Pritchard. He'll be arriving tomorrow afternoon."

"In that case," Dixie said, "he can have my prisoner with my full blessings."

"And ours as well," Morton said. "We're just sick and tired of all the dying. We hope that after those men failed to successfully loot my store, the word will get out to others of low character that robbers and murderers will fare very badly in Rio Paso."

"I'm sure that will be the case," Dixie assured the mayor.

"Uh-hem," one of the other men said, clearing his throat.

"Oh, yeah, Miss Ballou. We'd sort of like you to stay on here at the jail, and we've decided that we'd be willing to pay you a little something for that valuable service."

"Pay me?"

"Why not? You prevented a lynching last night."

"I had the doctor standing by my side," Dixie said, her voice faintly accusing. "He was the only one that did take a stand against rope justice."

Morton took a sudden interest in the floor, and his companions looked everywhere but at Dixie. Finally, Morton cleared his own throat and said, "A dollar a day and found, Miss Ballou. Is that acceptable?"

Dixie thought about it for a minute, then said, "Isn't there someone with experience around that would be a better choice as constable?"

"Frankly, no," Morton said. "We've discussed this matter to death, and you're the only one that we can agree upon to watch over the jail until Gus returns. Will you accept our proposition?"

Dixie thought hard about it. Finally, she said, "If I can train and exercise horses in the morning hours and I don't have to break up fights or—"

"All you would be expected to do is oversee this office and any prisoners."

"That's all?"

"That's all," Morton assured her. "Marshal Gus should be back soon, and we just need someone here that we can count on to do the right thing."

"Then I'll take the job until Gus returns," Dixie said with a smile.

The three town councilmen smiled, too, and then they excused themselves and left.

Dixie walked over to the cell and looked at Mitch. "You're pretty lucky. A sheriff's deputy will protect you, and a judge shouldn't give you more than a few years in prison. That's a whole lot better than lynch mob justice."

"Yeah," Mitch said, wringing his hands, "but I sure do hate to think of going to prison. I'd even rather farm."

"Then do it when you get out a free man," Dixie suggested. "Because as an outlaw, you're a big failure."

"I guess," Mitch said. Then, looking up, he added, "But out of the four of us drunk sonsaguns, I'm the only one that is still alive. That means I ain't all that unlucky."

Dixie had to smile because when you looked at it like that, Mitch was absolutely right.

Hugh was buried the next morning in a pauper's grave alongside his two fellow thieves, and no one attended except the grave digger and the undertaker. Later, when Dr. Ryder was laid to rest, more than a hundred people showed up to hear a eulogy and to watch.

"We're going to have to find us another sawbones," someone said, voicing a common concern. "Ain't likely we can find one as good as Ryder."

"Wonder who's bullet got him," another said with a sad shake of his head.

"Does it matter?"

Dixie knew that it did not matter. Dr. Ryder had been a fine man and an excellent physician. Now, because of a bunch of trigger-happy fools, he was gone. His demise would mean that the women of Rio Paso would not have the benefit of a doctor, nor would the children, or the men who got hurt at work.

"I don't think that I'll ever see you again," Mitch said when Dixie returned from the funeral. "I got a feeling that I'll never live to see Santa Fe, either."

"Of course you will," Dixie said, annoyed by the prisoner's whining. "Deputy Pritchard isn't going to let anything happen to you."

"I wish that I could believe that," Mitch said, looking like he was about to climb the gallows. "I just got a feeling that I'm going to go the same way as the others, straight to Boot Hill."

"You sure are a gloomy gus and a champion worrier."

Ten minutes later, an entourage composed of the mayor and the same members of the city council escorted a slender, dark-haired man into the marshal's office. He had a drooping mustache and cold gray eyes. His dress was rather more like what one would have expected of a gambler, or a professional gunfighter, instead of a sheriff's deputy. Pritchard wore the gun on his hip as if it were an extension of his own body.

"Miss Ballou," Morton said, looking uncomfortable, "this here is Deputy Pritchard."

The sheriff's officer extended his hand, and when they shook, Dixie did not feel any calluses. She wondered if Pritchard had ever done any real physical work and decided that he had not. Dixie believed that she had a good intuitive sense of character, and she did not like her gut feeling about the Santa Fe deputy.

The man smiled without warmth. "When they told me that you were living in Marshal Gus's office and they were actually paying you to be a jailer, I couldn't believe my ears. If that don't beat everything I ever heard! Hiring a fool girl to be your jailer!"

Morton and his town councilmen shifted with embarrassment as the deputy laughed in short little bursts that made the hairs on Dixie's neck stand on end.

She bristled. "You look like a dude, Deputy Pritchard. Or a two-bit gunslinger."

"Miss Ballou!" Morton protested. "I assure you that Deputy Pritchard is being very accommodating. He dropped everything to come here and take this prisoner off our hands."

"That's right," the lawman snarled. "And as for looks, you remind me of a boy."

Dixie's fists balled at her sides. "Why don't you just take the prisoner and leave?"

"That's my intention, Miss Jailer."

Dixie wished that Ruff had been in the room. He would have handed this arrogant jackass his teeth.

"Miss Ballou," their prisoner cried, looking frightened half to death. "I'd rather take my chances with a lynch mob than with that deputy."

"Shut up," Pritchard ordered. "Girl, where are the damn cell keys?"

"Here," Dixie said, not at all happy with the way things were unfolding. "But you must promise to change the bandage on this man's shoulder and make sure that his bullet wound doesn't reopen."

"I don't got to do anything," the deputy hissed, marching over to the cell and unlocking the door. He drew his six-gun, pointed it at the cowering prisoner, and said, "Put your hands over your damned head and march!"

Mitch threw up his good arm, but he couldn't get the right one up because of his shoulder wound. The deputy decided that he needed help and jumped inside the cell. He grabbed Mitch's right arm and jerked it overhead.

"Ahhhh!" Mitch screamed, collapsing in pain.

Dixie had seen more than enough. She snatched up her own gun and shouted, "Deputy Pritchard, get away from my prisoner!"

Pritchard turned, saw the gun in Dixie's hand, and froze as she cocked back the hammer and said, "Get out of my cell."

"Are you crazy!"

"Move the barrel of that gun another inch in my direction and find out."

Pritchard turned to the mayor for help. "Are you gonna do something, or what!"

"Miss Ballou . . ."

"I won't turn my prisoner over to this man," Dixie said. "Look at how badly the deputy has already hurt him!"

Mitch was a quivering, whimpering mass. His left hand was splayed across the bandage on his right shoulder, which was soaking with fresh blood.

"Mayor, I think you'd better order Deputy Pritchard to return to Santa Fe right now," Dixie warned. "Either that, or we're going to have another funeral."

Morton looked to the other town councilmen, but they quickly glanced away. The mayor of Rio Paso pleaded to Dixie with his eyes, but she remained steadfast, gun riveted on Pritchard, who was quaking with barely suppressed rage.

Finally, Morton blurted, "There's been too much killing in Rio Paso already, Deputy Pritchard. I think you'd better go on back to Santa Fe."

"Why, you gutless son of a bitch! Are you going to let a tomboy order us around!"

"She's got the gun, Deputy."

Pritchard looked ready to explode. He tried to stare Dixie down. Failing that, he cursed, then holstered his gun and charged out the door yelling, "Don't expect me to ever come back here the next time Rio Paso needs help!"

Dixie waited only as long as it took the man to leave the office, then she dashed into the cell, knowing that she had to get the shoulder wound to stop hemorrhaging or Mitch would bleed to death for sure.

"Morton, find me some bandages!"

"You shouldn't have done that, Miss Ballou."

"Now!"

"Yes'm!"

"He'd have killed me," Mitch whimpered as he rocked back and forth on the floor of his cell. "All I had to do was to look into that son of a bitch's eyes and I knew that he would have made sure that I never reached Santa Fe."

"I know," Dixie said. "Now, let's get your shirt off and see if we can repair the damage."

Mitch nodded weakly, and then he fainted.

SIXTEEN

Dixie had to work frantically to get her prisoner's shoulder wound to stop bleeding. She didn't know how much blood Mitch lost, but it was much too much. The young man was as white as mashed potatoes, and his pulse was weak.

"You're going to need a lot of rest," Dixie said when she finally had the bleeding under control and a new bandage in place. "I wish to heavens I could do something more for you, but I can't. I've searched Dr. Ryder's medical kit and office for more laudanum, and there doesn't seem to be any."

"How about some whiskey?" Mitch whispered. "Just enough to cut the pain. I sure ain't in no shape to get drunk and rowdy, and this ain't no saloon."

"All right," Dixie decided. "We could both use some."

She took one of the bottles out of Marshal Gus's drawer and found two glasses, which she polished clean. Having half filled each, she handed one to Mitch and said, "Drink this."

Mitch drank, and it seemed to help, because some of his color returned. The whiskey was awful, but Dixie drank a couple of fingers full, and it made her feel better also.

"I can't imagine a man like Pritchard being a law officer," Dixie said, sitting down next to her prisoner and placing the bottle and glasses between them.

"He'd have killed me for certain," Mitch said. "I could see that the minute I laid eyes upon him."

144

"Me, too." Dixie splashed whiskey into each of their glasses. "Well, I need sleep."

Mitch reached out and touched Dixie's cheek. "You saved my life again, Miss Ballou. There ain't no way that I can ever thank you."

"Forget it," Dixie said, pushing his hand aside. "You're still my prisoner, and you're half-dead from the loss of blood."

"I'm going to make it now," Mitch vowed. "And I've decided that I'll just have to take my medicine and go to prison. But when I come out, I promise I'll never make the same kind of mistakes I used to. I'm going to find a new line of work. Something with a future."

"That's a good idea." Dixie was quiet for a moment, and then she said, "Have you ever worked with horses?"

"Sure."

"Maybe you could be a teamster or a blacksmith. Something like that."

"I'd rather go mustanging," Mitch said before emptying his glass. "I like the excitement and the freedom."

"Do you enjoy horses?"

"Why sure, Miss Ballou! I like 'em a lot. Next to the ladies, there ain't nothing near so pretty."

Dixie thought of the insults heaped upon her by the deputy from Santa Fe. "I guess that I do look like a tomboy, huh?"

"Oh, no, Miss Ballou! You're real pretty. Prettiest girl I've seen in a while."

"Since yesterday, I'll bet."

Mitch shook his head. The whiskey was definitely reviving him. "Miss Ballou, there are plenty of women in this part of the country. Most are wives or mothers, some are soiled doves, and some are just plain rough and ready. But a girl like you is . . . is like a flower in a field of weeds. She just sort of sticks out and catches your eye."

"I do?" Dixie asked shamelessly.

"Fer sure," Mitch said. "I've messed up my life already, but if things were different and I had something to offer, I'd be callin' on you every chance."

Dixie was warmed by his compliment and also by the whiskey. "I'm just sorry that you ever got into this mess."

"Me, too."

"More whiskey?"

"No, thank you. Whiskey is my downfall."

"I forgot."

Dixie climbed to her feet and walked to the cell door. "I know that you're not going anywhere, but I'm going to lock up just the same."

"That's fine with me," Mitch said. "In fact, I rest easier knowing that nobody can get in here without you lettin' 'em."

Dixie corked the bottle and placed it in a drawer before lying down on her bunk. She was bone-tired, and it was only a few minutes until she was asleep.

Wong Woo awakened Dixie and her prisoner that evening and brought them in a couple of heaping trays of food, which was as delicious as always.

The mayor came by about eight o'clock and knocked on the front door. "Miss Ballou, everything is quiet," he said, not bothering to come inside but preferring to remain out on the walkway.

"That's a comfort to know."

"It's a comfort to all of us," Morton said. "I've been walking around town, and there's no more of that crazy lynching talk being spread around the saloons."

"I'm very glad to hear that. Did Bob Justin and his cowboys return to the Rocking J Ranch?"

"Yes."

Dixie expelled a sigh. "I'm glad to hear that, too."

"How are you and the prisoner holding up?"

"We're doing fine."

Morton frowned. "Miss Ballou, it's only fair to tell you that we're going to have to wait until the circuit judge comes through Rio Paso before we can have the trial."

"How long might that be?"

"Couple of weeks."

Dixie didn't mind. "I'm not going anyplace until my brother returns."

"Good," Morton said with a grin. "I've been thinking about what happened with that Santa Fe deputy, and I agree that he was a bad one. I'm glad that we didn't let him take our prisoner. And, if it's any comfort, I can tell you that the other members of the town council feel the same way."

"It is a comfort."

"Good night, Miss Ballou."

Dixie closed the door, and Mitch called from his cell in an anxious voice, "Who was that?"

"It was the mayor," Dixie explained. "He just wanted to assure me that everything was quiet on the street and in the saloons. There will be no trouble."

"Whew! That's a relief."

Dixie opened the cell and went inside to collect her prisoner's dinner plate. "How is the shoulder feeling?"

"A lot better."

"Good."

Dixie had turned and started back out of the cell when the front door to the marshal's office burst open. Deputy Pritchard slammed the door shut behind him, a wolfish grin on his face.

"You!" Dixie cried, slinging the dinner tray with its

empty dishes at the Santa Fe deputy.

Pritchard jumped sideways and avoided the tray. In three long strides he crossed the marshal's office and intercepted Dixie, who was leaping for her six-gun.

"Ouch!" Dixie cried as the edge of Pritchard's palm chopped down against her forearm, paralyzing it and causing her to drop the six-gun.

"Hey!" Mitch shouted. "Don't hurt her!"

Pritchard wasn't listening. The back of his hand came flying up to strike Dixie's face. She staggered and fell, her head striking the floor. She must have lost consciousness for a moment, because, when she regained her senses, she was being dragged into the jail and Mitch was cowering against the wall.

"All right, prisoner, stick out your hands!"

"Huh?"

"Stick 'em out!" Pritchard growled.

"I ain't goin' anywhere with you!" Mitch cried, pressing against the cell's far wall with his left fist cocked.

"Is that right?" The deputy shrugged, drew his six-gun, and attacked, the barrel of the gun easily breaking through Mitch's feeble defenses.

Dixie saw the young man stagger, blood pouring out of his broken nose. A second whipping dropped Mitch to his knees, and the prisoner tried to cover his head, but the deputy hit him twice more.

Dixie was coming to her feet when Pritchard stepped back out of the cell and grabbed her by the hair. He jerked her head back and growled, "Did you really think I'd let a damned tomboy send me draggin' back to Santa Fe with my tail tucked between my legs!"

Dixie tried to claw Pritchard's eyes out, but he threw her against the wall and struck her across the top of the head with the barrel of his pistol. After that, Dixie didn't remember anything until the next morning, when she awoke to the sound of Wong Woo beating impatiently on her door.

"Mr. Woo," she groaned. "Help me!"

Dixie saw the door handle turn a little, and she realized that the Chinaman was trying to get in but that the door was bolted shut.

"Help!" she cried, her head feeling as if it had been split open with an axe.

But her voice was hoarse, her cry barely a whisper, and after a few moments, Wong Woo must have left, because there was nothing but silence.

Dixie crawled to the cell door and used it to pull herself erect. She clung to the bars, her head swirling and her eyes unfocused.

"Help, someone!"

Dixie closed her eyes, fighting off the pain, and she tried to push the door of the cell open, but it was locked. She sank down to her knees, leaned forward, and tried to gather her senses. She wasn't sure how long she remained like that before someone else came to knock on the front door.

"Miss Ballou! Are you in there!"

"Morton?" Dixie lifted her head, and a stabbing pain made her gasp. "Help!"

It was several minutes before she heard the sound of a sledge striking the front door. Each blow sent spikes through her brain, and when the door was finally smashed open, a crowd rushed inside.

"Miss Ballou!" Morton shouted, trying to yank open the door and finding it locked. "What happened?"

Dixie told them about the Santa Fe deputy bursting into her office and how he'd beaten her and then taken her wounded and unconscious prisoner by force. She ended by asking, "What time is it?"

"It's nine o'clock."

Dixie groaned. "Mitch could already be dead!"

"Now, Miss Ballou, maybe there's just been some terrible mistake," the mayor said as people finally found the extra key to the jail cell and set Dixie free. "I can't believe that a deputy would behave so despicably."

"Mistake?" Dixie looked up. "Do you think I made this all up?"

"No, but . . . well, maybe your prisoner got the drop on you and . . . well, if he got away, we'll form up a posse and catch him."

"He didn't get away!" Dixie cried. "He was beaten just like I was and dragged out of this cell."

"Why don't you get her over to the marshal's bunk and let her rest?" the mayor said in a condescending voice. "It's clear that she's hurt and confused."

But Dixie was having none of that. Her head was still pounding, but it was also clearing. "Get away from me!" she exclaimed. "I've got to overtake them. Will anyone come with me?"

When no one volunteered, Dixie looked for her six-gun, which she remembered had been knocked flying. Unable to find it, she went over to the rifle rack and removed a Winchester.

"Miss Ballou, please! Won't you just calm down and let's talk some sense into all this craziness!"

But Dixie was finished with talk. "I'm going after that Pritchard and my prisoner," she announced. "And I just pray that Mitch is still alive."

Dixie closed her ears to their protests. She was wobbly but managed to get past them and outside. She was reeling by the time that she arrived at the livery with the idea of taking up Deputy Pritchard's trail back to Santa Fe.

"Hey!" a voice shouted from up the street. "What the hell are you doing!"

Dixie ground her teeth, intending to ignore the challenge. But then something clicked inside of her like the tumblers in a lock falling precisely into place.

Dixie's jaw dropped, then snapped shut. She drew a hand shakily across her eyes, wondering if the whipping she'd taken had damaged something in her head.

But no, it was he! It was Houston, and he was riding a . . . a Missouri mule! A joyful cry filled Dixie's throat, and she took two racing steps forward before her knees buckled and the world spun her back into darkness.

SEVENTEEN

Houston looked down at his kid sister and smiled. "Dixie? Dixie wake up."

Her eyelids fluttered, but she did not awaken, and so he accepted the wet compress from the mayor's hand and gently laid it across Dixie's brow. Houston's lean, handsome face was burned dark, the color of mahogany. Although he was only twenty-two years old, the federal prison he'd survived had aged his appearance so dramatically that he looked ten years older.

His eyes revealed both pain and suffering, and only his hands remained unchanged by his long federal imprisonment as a Confederate spy. They were uncommonly graceful for so large and rugged a man. He'd inherited them from his Cherokee mother, and more than one foolish jokester had paid with his teeth for making fun of Houston's long, tapered fingers—fingers that were extraordinary at manipulating a deck of cards, a gun, or the body of a beautiful woman.

"Who did this to her?" Houston asked no one in particular as he stared at Dixie's battered face. "Who laid a hand on my kid sister?"

"It was the sheriff of Santa Fe's deputy," the mayor nervously explained. "His name is Pritchard. He came to take our prisoner, but Miss Ballou didn't trust him so she ordered Pritchard back to Santa Fe."

"That's right," Mayor Morton said. "We decided to keep the prisoner here until the circuit judge comes around."

"And this . . . this Pritchard, he took your prisoner by force?"

Morton gulped. "Yeah. That's what Miss Ballou claimed. I dunno, it seems real hard to believe that a deputy would act that way and then—"

Houston didn't even look up from his sister's face as his large and graceful hand flashed upward to grab the mayor by his collar and drag his horse face down to eye level.

"Sir, are you suggesting that Dixie was lying about that deputy and her prisoner?"

Morton couldn't breathe, and his eyes bugged with terror when Houston said, "Is that what you are suggesting, sir?"

"No!" Morton choked, shaking his head feebly.

The corners of Houston's mouth lifted just a fraction of an inch, and he released the mayor, who staggered backward. Houston twisted around on the bed to which he'd carried Dixie, and regarded the other townspeople. "What about my brother?" he asked them as a group.

Their eyes snapped back and forth, each of them waiting for someone else to speak, all of them afraid they might suffer the same fate as their still-gagging mayor.

"For the last time," Houston said without a trace of anger, "before someone gets hurt. What happened to Mr. Rufus Ballou?"

"My name is Amos Culbert," a portly man wheezed, sweating furiously. "I really like and admire your brother. He and Miss Ballou shot the hell outa a bunch of bank robbers the very first day they came to Rio Paso. Then Marshal Gus and your brother went after them robbers."

"There was only one surviving bank robber," another merchant quickly amended. "Miss Ballou and Mr. Rufus, they killed the other three. The last one, he joined up with some other men and they ambushed our posse. Gunned down some real fine boys."

"And that," Houston said, "is when your marshal and my brother went after them?"

"Yes, sir!"

Houston was quiet for a moment, his expression contemplative. No one in the room even breathed, and they all watched his big hand to make sure that it did not stray nearer to the worn Colt on his hip.

"We was payin' your sister a dollar a day just to mind the jail and look after that prisoner until either our own marshal returned or the judge came around," Culbert explained. "Miss Dixie seemed to need the money, and we thought it would help all the way around."

"That's right," another said. "Your sister, she was going to have the mornings off to ride horses for folks hereabouts. She rode a bucking horse to a standstill out on our main street. Nobody has ever seen the likes of that ride, not even the local cowboys."

"Dixie is only fifteen years old," Houston said, his eyes frosting and his voice taking on a knife edge. "Didn't it ever occur to any of you grown men to take care of your own prisoners?"

Culbert glanced at the others, some of whom actually bolted out the door. Tearing a big handkerchief and mopping his face, Culbert stammered, "Your sister didn't have much money. The bucking horse she rode busted a wagon tongue and did some damage that she needed to pay for. The prisoner was just a kid, and badly wounded at that. There wasn't any risk, Mr. Ballou. Honest! We thought we were doing the right thing."

Houston forced himself to relax. "You're telling me that a sheriff's deputy from Santa Fe slapped the hell out of my kid sister?"

"Well, yes, sir, but . . ."

"And how many men from this town are riding after this deputy and the wounded prisoner?"

Culbert bit his lower lip and squirmed under Houston's hard gaze. "Well, I ain't the mayor! I just run a little shop down the street."

Houston signaled for a basin of cool water to be brought closer. A man did so, but acted as if he were offering fresh meat to a famished lion and was afraid of getting his hand bitten off.

"Get out of here," Houston said, wetting the rag again and swabbing his sister's bruised face.

Dixie's eyelashes fluttered again, and Houston expelled a deep sigh of relief before he looked up and growled, "You people all make me sick."

Culbert and several of the others grabbed the still-incapacitated mayor and stampeded out the door. When they were gone, Houston looked down at his sister, hating the purplish bruises that marred her pretty and innocent young face.

"I guess things haven't gone real well for you and Ruff, either," he said to his unconscious sister. "Well, the war is over, the South is lost, but at least what is left of us Ballous are together again."

Houston walked over to his saddlebags and extracted a silver flask. He uncorked it and took a long drink. His eyes closed for a moment as he savored the all too familiar fire in his throat.

What a long, hard trail it had been to Rio Paso. He'd always hoped that he would find his brother and sister alive and prospering. Well, at least they were still alive.

"Houston?"

He pivoted on his heel and hurried to the bedside. Taking Dixie's hands in his own, he squeezed them tightly. "How are you doing?"

"I've felt better and I've felt worse. But seeing you again is about as wonderful as anything I can imagine."

Houston was not ordinarily a demonstrative man. But now his eyes glistened. "It's been a long, hard time, Dixie. There were days in a federal prison when I expected I'd never see freedom again. Never see your pretty face."

"What about Molly O'Day?" Dixie dared to ask. "Did she come west with you?"

Houston's eyes filled with tears, and they slid down his tanned cheeks. "Molly died trying to escape a federal prison," he whispered, bitterness thick in his voice.

"I'm sorry," Dixie said, feeling as if Pritchard had punched her in the throat, because it ached so badly. "Miss O'Day was a brave woman."

"She was everything to me," Houston said, roughly wiping a sleeve across his eyes. "If I could kill the Yanks that were responsible for her death, I'd gladly give up my own life."

"I know you would, Houston, but that wouldn't bring her back, and now *we* need you."

"I wouldn't even have found you except that everywhere I went, people remembered our stallions. And then when I saw old High Man, I knew I'd found you and Ruff at last."

Dixie reached up and touched the damp rag he had laid so neatly across her forehead. "We've got to overtake that deputy before he kills Mitch."

"The prisoner?"

"Yes."

"Uh-uh," Houston said. "We're going after Ruff. I don't give a damn about the prisoner."

"But he'll be killed if we don't help him."

"He's a thief," Houston said. "We need to find Ruff."

"Ruff is with Marshal Gus. He'll be all right," Dixie

argued. "Please, Houston. I've got to try and save that poor man."

Houston's jaw muscles corded, and he was silent for a moment before he reasoned out loud, "If I say yes and we go after your prisoner, you must promise me one thing."

"Anything you say."

"All right, promise me that when we come upon this Deputy Pritchard, you'll stay out of my way and not make a fuss no matter what happens."

"You can't kill a sheriff's deputy!" Dixie's head rolled back and forth on her pillow. "Houston, if you kill a lawman, even a bad one, you'll be a hunted man. Our name will be stained again no matter how just the punishment."

"You promised."

"Houston, please! You don't *need* to kill him."

The corners of Houston's eyes tightened, and more tears leaked out. He angrily scrubbed them away with his sleeve. "And what happens if this Santa Fe deputy attempts to kill me?"

Dixie didn't need to think twice before answering. "Then defend yourself."

"Fair enough," Houston said. "How soon will you be fit to travel?"

"In about an hour. Saddle High Man and saddle a mare I named Aria. She's a tall sorrel with flaxen mane and tail, crooked blaze, and as pretty a conformation as you'll ever find."

"All right," Houston said. "It'll be good not to have to ride a mule anymore, though I confess I have taken somewhat of a shine to him."

"When I saw you on a mule, it really caught me by surprise," Dixie said. "How in the world did you, of all people, end up riding a mule!"

"Won him playing cards," Houston explained. "He's a good traveler and the smartest thing that I ever rode. His name is Geezer and we've come to terms. I treat him with respect and feed him grain, and he don't try to kill me or fake a lameness. We've traveled all the way from Memphis together, and we've had our share of scrapes and hard times."

"But . . . a mule?"

"A man has to ride what he owns," Houston said, looking a little embarrassed. "And I expect that I'll probably sell him now that I've got horses again."

"I expect you should," Dixie said. "You're a Ballou."

"I know." Houston got up to leave. "Dixie?"

"Yes?"

"It won't change things if Deputy Pritchard delivers your prisoner to Santa Fe in good shape."

Houston's eyes tightened as he studied the unsightly welt across Dixie's otherwise pretty face. "Do you understand?"

"I do."

"Good, because I just want you to know what I aim to do to the man as payback."

"Houston, just don't kill him and give our family a bad reputation out west. Because there is nowhere else for us to go."

"Sure," he said after a long moment of deliberation. And then he turned and left to saddle their horses for the trail to Santa Fe.

Dixie shook her head with wonder. Imagine Houston finding them after so long. Her heart ached for the pain she read in Houston's eyes when he spoke of Miss O'Day. Molly had been a beautiful woman, fiery, bright, and high spirited. She'd been irresistible to men, and Dixie knew that her brother had fallen head over heels in love with Molly from the very first moment they'd met. Dixie felt a pang of guilt to remember how she'd first thought of Molly as scatterbrained and weak. It was now clear that Molly's helpless act had been necessary to hide the woman's devotion to the South and to fool important Northerners into thinking her incapable of intrigue.

The important thing now was that Houston not be consumed by hatred for ex-Yankees who'd come west and had a foolish tendency to crow about the defeat of the Confederacy. There were many such men in the West, and there had often been times that it had been extremely difficult for her and Ruff not to react with harsh words that could have led to violence. Lord knew that things were violent enough in the West without reenacting all the old hatreds that would long exist between the North and the South.

It is time for peace and for healing, Dixie thought. Time we had a second chance as a family of Western horsemen.

Dixie was feeling pretty wobbly when she mounted Aria a short time later. The mare was excited, and especially so in the presence of old High Man, who bowed his head, snorted, and generally acted about half his age.

"Settle down," Houston ordered the old stallion. "This isn't a parade and we aren't going to the races."

Dixie had her hands full with the high-strung sorrel mare, and Roscoe looked worried. "Your color ain't none too good, Dixie. You should be in bed, not on a high-flying mare."

"Maybe you should ride Geezer, my mule," Houston said, taking a closer look at his sister and realizing that Dixie did look unnaturally pale.

"I wouldn't be caught dead on a mule. Besides, we have a lot of catching up to do."

But when Aria spun around and almost unseated Dixie, she knew that she was not fit enough to ride the animal. "Why don't we trade horses?" she suggested. "This mare is a handful, and I know that High Man will settle down as soon as we get moving."

"Suits me," Houston said, dismounting.

They had also to switch saddles, and when they were ready to ride, Dixie said, "Roscoe, don't you worry about us paying you for the feed. We'll come up with the money, and that's a promise."

"If you can't," the old man said, "I'll take that Missouri mule in trade instead of one of your Thoroughbreds."

"Now why," Dixie asked, "would you be willing to do something as foolish as that?"

"Because he's a damned handsome mule," Roscoe explained. "And I like 'em better than horses. Always have. A mule is either the best animal you ever handled, or the worst. Not much in between. And Houston's mule is a good 'un."

The compliment pleased Houston immensely. He actually smiled. "I'm glad to hear you say that. I was trying to explain to my sister the advantages of a mule, but of course, she wouldn't listen."

"Your sister is as fine a horsewoman as I've ever seen, so that shouldn't surprise any of us. Oh, I almost forgot."

"Forgot what?" Dixie said.

"Mr. Benson came by with his men last evening, and when he saw your Thoroughbreds, he wanted to know how much you'd take for a couple of the mares, including the one that your brother is fixin' to ride."

"Aria is not for sale."

"Mr. Benson has a nice stallion that he thinks would cross real well with your mares."

Dixie bristled, remembering how grieving and vindictive old man Benson had threatened to get even with Marshal Gus for not doing his job. "I wouldn't even sell my brother's mule to that hate-filled old man."

"Well," Roscoe said, "that's too bad because you and your brothers do need the money. Anyway, I said I'd mention it to you while Mr. Benson and his men were off to Alder Creek to take up the trail of them ambushers."

Dixie stiffened. "They are?"

"Yep. That old man said he was tired of waiting on Marshal Gus to bring in his son's killer. Said he reckoned he would handle the matter hisself."

Houston must have read the sudden concern in Dixie's face, because he mounted Aria and said, "Trouble?"

"Could be," Dixie said. "Mr. Benson blames Marshal Gus for the death of his son. I hope he's calmed down enough to be reasonable and understand that it was his son's own fault that Charlie died in an ambush."

"Maybe we should forget about Santa Fe. Especially if Ruff's life is at stake."

Dixie had to stretch a little to get her boot into High Man's stirrup. The stallion, unlike Aria, stood rooted until Dixie was firmly seated. "It won't take us long to find Deputy Pritchard and make sure that his prisoner arrives in Santa Fe. After that, we'll ride for Alder Creek and take up the ambushers' trail."

"Are you sure?" Houston asked, looking doubtful.

Dixie wasn't sure, but she nodded her head anyway. If this delay on account of Mitch cost Ruff his life, she would never forgive herself. On the other hand, Dixie felt strongly about her obligation to protect her prisoner from abuse and possible murder. She hadn't been wearing a badge when Deputy Pritchard barged into the marshal's office, knocked her half-silly, and then callously taken Mitch by force. But badge or no badge, it had been the wrong thing to do and Pritchard was a very bad lawman who needed a very good lesson in justice.

EIGHTEEN

They rode late into the evening and made camp along the banks of the Rio Grande. Dixie, still feeling the effects of the backhanded blow she'd taken from Deputy Pritchard, was experiencing a severe headache, and when she touched her face, she could feel the swelling.

"Here," Houston said, coming back from the river with a cool compress. "I wish we had some ice for your face. Do you want a shot of whiskey?"

"Maybe a little," she said, accepting the flask from her brother. "Ruff and I were always thinking about you. We were afraid that you might even be dead."

"After I heard that Molly was shot to death while trying to escape, I thought that I would die," Houston confessed, staring into their little camp fire. "Things were real bad in the federal prison. There were almost twenty-two thousand of us prisoners of war penned and guarded outdoors like animals. We never had enough food or blankets, and some of our rebel boys were shot up and some just either went crazy or took their own lives."

"I'm sorry."

Houston leaned closer to the fire, passing his hands back and forth across the flames, whose lights danced across his staring eyes.

"Houston, let's not talk about the war."

But Houston wasn't listening. "I remember last winter," he said, speaking to himself, "we were so cold. There was never anything to burn. When men lost hope, some of them would die, but a few would burn their clothes late at night just to be warm for an hour or so, and then they'd lay down and freeze to death."

Houston shook his head in wonder. "Dixie, they'd just go to sleep. Early the next morning, we'd see them, and they'd look so peaceful lying on the frozen ground, often covered with a shroud of glistening snow or frost."

"Houston, I wish you wouldn't think about such things."

"It's all right," he said, waving his hands back and forth across the flames, "because those frozen corpses always bore a . . . a soft smile. They looked like they were caught and frozen in a happy dream."

"Houston, please," Dixie begged, moving over beside him and taking his arms and pulling his hands away from the flames. "It's done. You have to put it all out of your mind."

He finally looked at her. "I don't rightly know that I ever can do that."

"You have to try."

"I suppose," he said, not really sounding as if he believed it. Turning back to the flames, he caught her by surprise when he said, "Aren't you even wondering what's left of our home in Tennessee?"

"No." Dixie shook her head violently. "I don't ever want to hear about it. That's past."

"It's also gone," Houston said. "Everything is gone, and there's nothing left but ghosts and graves. I spent just one night there, but I saw—"

"We're going to find land out here," Dixie said loudly, her voice high and anxious as she overrode her brother. "Ruff and I have been looking everywhere for a place to settle. We had Cherokee land in the Indian Territory, up near the Oklahoma and Kansas border."

"I know. You wrote about it in a letter you and Ruff sent to Aunt Maybelle."

"Then she actually received our letters and saved them for you?"

"Yes, her plantation was the first place I thought of after leaving what little remained of Wildwood. I knew Aunt Maybelle would still be there and she'd know where I could find you and Ruff."

"But I didn't believe she'd get the letter we sent from Texas or the one from—"

"I got 'em all in my saddlebags. In your last letter, you said you were following the Rio Grande, probably all the way up to Colorado. I hooked up with some hiders, and we came straight across the Comanche country. We was jumped but fought our way through, and when I reached old Santa Fe, they remembered you and Ruff and the Thoroughbreds. People who saw you on them horses always remembered, Dixie."

"Seeing you again is a miracle." Dixie hugged her brother. "But I'm scared more than ever now."

"No need for that."

"We thought sure you were dead."

"I'm alive, but sometimes, late at night, I feel dead."

"It'll pass, Houston, it'll pass."

Dixie studied Houston's lean face, hating how much he had aged. When last she'd seen him riding north to find and help Molly, there had been some boyishness left in her oldest living brother. But the federal prison had replaced that with hard, uncompromising angles, lines, and ridges. Houston was still a fine enough figure of manhood to turn a woman's head, but now he bore a trace of something a little frightening.

"They pardoned us the day after General Lee's surrender

at Appomattox Courthouse," Houston said without pre-
amble. "I wasn't supposed to be set free on account of
being a spy. But when they opened the prison gates, we
charged the guards, waving our hands and screaming at the
top of our lungs. They either had to shoot us down or let us
pass, and they decided to let us pass. We just kept running
and running."

Houston reached for his flask and drank hard, then offered
it to Dixie, who took a pull. Houston took seconds on the
flask. "Dixie, I never ran so long or so hard as I did the day
they opened the gates to that prison. When my legs finally
quit, there wasn't no one left to run past me. I jumped into
a river and let it carry me away."

"You could have caught pneumonia. At this time of
year, the rivers are still very cold."

"I didn't feel anything," Houston said. "I floated two
days on a log, eating fish and frogs and watching the sky
and the trees. The river was runnin' south. I stole a nice
big flatboat, ran her downriver for two days, and sold it
for thirty dollars. I took that money to a card game and
won some traveling money and my mule, Geezer. I believe
it was in North Carolina, though all of the South looks shot
to hell."

Dixie did not want to hear about the South. She wanted
it to remain in her memory as proud, untrampled, and
unsullied by the damned Yankee armies. "Houston," she
said quickly, "everyone says that Denver is beautiful and
there is good, cheap land just to its east."

"I don't know if I can stop moving," he said. "Moving
helps me forget the past."

Dixie pushed on. "The three of us are going to build a
horse ranch even bigger and better than Wildwood Farm.
We've still got High Man and High Fire, and we've got

some new Thoroughbred mares, including the one you're riding. It's going to be just the way that Father would have wanted."

"I miss the Blue Ridge Mountains sometimes so much that I could shout," Houston said, his knuckles white from clenching his flask. "And fireflies, Dixie. Have you noticed that they don't have fireflies out west? I've been looking, but you'll never see one. No dogwood or red cardinals."

"There's other things! Big land. Tall pines. Sunsets and sunrises that flow like liquid gold across the mountains. There are wild mustangs and burros and mountain lions. You'll see eagles and hawks and wolves and buffalo."

Houston nodded at the flames. "I learned from the hiders that if you see buffalo, there might be Comanche and Kiowa close and you'd better get your rifle and stay awake at night."

Dixie couldn't reach her brother. "I'm sorry," she said, "for everything."

Houston drank the flask empty. After a long while, he said, "You were right about not killing Deputy Pritchard, because we haven't any damned place left to go."

"Let's sleep. Sleep will help."

But Houston wouldn't budge. He just sat and watched the fire die as Dixie fell asleep worrying if her brother had already lost a part of his soul as well as his heart.

They found a fresh grave the following morning just after sunrise. It was unmarked and there wasn't even a mound. But you could see that it was a grave and it was fresh.

"What do you want to do?" Houston asked. "There's a good chance that it might not belong to your prisoner."

"And at least as good a chance that it does," Dixie said, dismounting and handing her reins to her brother before she knelt at the edge of the grave.

Houston also dismounted. "Get back on your horse," Houston ordered. "Now."

"Still the bossy one," she said, remounting Aria. "You always did like to give the orders."

Houston didn't say anything as he started to dig. He didn't have to dig very far. Less than two feet down he touched the body and recoiled. Then, steeling himself, Houston drove his hand deeper into the freshly turned earth until he felt something.

"Got his arm," Houston said, pulling.

Dixie turned away. She couldn't help it.

"This fella's shoulder is all bandaged up," Houston said a few moments later. "He looks real young, but his nose is busted and . . . and there's two bullet holes in his chest."

"That's Mitch," Dixie whispered. "That damned Pritchard must have lost his temper and shot him to death. Mitch was half-dead already when he was carried from his cell."

"Shall I cover the kid back up?"

"No," Dixie finally whispered, hating herself because she didn't have the courage to turn and look at Mitch. "Get him out, and let's wrap him in a blanket and take him down to Santa Fe, where they'll bury him proper."

"You sure?"

"Yes."

And so it was done. Dixie could not look at the kid, and Aria had fits when they tied the stiff and battered corpse across her saddle. Dixie and Houston rode their Ballou stallion double the rest of the way down to old Santa Fe.

Santa Fe had been founded by the Spanish, who had originally named their new capital city La Villa Real de Santa Fe de San Francisco de Asis—the Royal City of the

Holy Faith of St. Francis of Assisi. Situated at the base of the Santa Fe River's exit from the Sangre de Cristo foothills, the town was built around a plaza, beside which still stood the impressive Palace of the Governors. The old city boasted crumbling adobe walls that were never able to keep out the marauding Apache during the first century of its existence.

Four flags had already flown over Santa Fe, belonging to Spain, Mexico, the Confederate States of America, and now America for the second time. The city had a rich tradition of Franciscan priests, trappers, and explorers, as well as teamsters, cowboys, and vaqueros from the many big ranches nearby. Its Mexican population was bold and colorful, and many parts of Old Santa Fe were a maze of narrow streets, impressive pueblos, and wild cantinas where a man could get tequila, whiskey, or women, depending on his tastes and the size of his wallet.

"The sheriff's office is downtown," Houston said as they weaved through the narrow, crowded streets.

"Remember what you promised," Dixie reminded her brother. "No killing."

"I'll remember."

When they reined up at the hitching rail before the sheriff's office, a sizable crowd gathered about them, attracted by the morbid spectacle of a body quite obviously disinterred from the grave.

"Why don't you morbid sonsabitches go find something better to do than stare at a dead man?" Houston growled, unloosing the blanket-shrouded body and dipping his shoulder under it. "Lead the way, Dixie."

"We're going right into the sheriff's office?"

"You got a better idea?"

"No."

"Then come on! I don't much enjoy toting this poor fella around. He might start leaking on me, and I've no money for new clothes."

Dixie hurried up to the sheriff's door. Without knocking, she went inside, and when Pritchard saw her, he almost catapulted over backward in his haste to get out of his chair. "What the hell!"

Houston bulled inside the office. There were three lawmen now on their feet, all of them gaping as Houston dumped the dirt-crusted blanket and its corpse on a desk.

"Which one is Pritchard?" Houston asked before anyone could think to speak.

"That one," Dixie said, pointing an accusing finger.

Houston's hand flashed to his six-gun, and it came up quicker than the blink of an eye, cocked and trained on Pritchard, who began to rapidly backpedal until he was blocked by one of two iron-barred cells.

"Jezus!" The oldest of the three exploded. "Stranger, do you want to take a moment to explain just what the hell is going on here!"

"Who are you?" Houston demanded, his eyes never leaving the deputy.

"Sheriff Holden! Who the hell are you?"

Dixie spoke up quickly. "I'm Miss Dixie Ballou, and this is my brother."

For the first time, Dixie forced herself to glance at the corpse now lying stiffly on the sheriff's desk. "And that was my prisoner. The one that you sent Deputy Pritchard to bring back here for trial."

The sheriff glanced sideways in question at Pritchard. "You said that the authorities in Rio Paso insisted on keeping the prisoner."

"They did!"

"That's right," Dixie said, "but your deputy took it upon himself to take my prisoner by force. He locked me in my cell, but not before he whipped the prisoner senseless with a pistol. Not twenty miles north of here, he shot our prisoner to death."

"Can you prove any of this?" the sheriff demanded.

"Damn right we can," Houston said, grabbing an edge of the blanket and yanking on it so hard that the corpse rolled over twice before tumbling off the desk to strike the floor with a loud and sickening thud. "You can see two bullet holes in the man's chest, and you can see what is left of his face after your deputy's whipping."

The sheriff gaped at Mitch's face and grew pale. He turned to the second deputy, who also looked stunned. "Sidney, get that thing over to the mortician's office, right now!"

"I ain't touching it!" Sidney cried.

"Do as I say!"

"No," Houston said quietly as he gauged the measure of Pritchard. "I want *him* to carry the body over to the mortician's office."

"The hell you say."

Houston took a deep breath, and then he holstered his six-gun. "I promised my sister that I wouldn't kill you. But you damn sure deserve to die."

"Now, wait just a minute," the sheriff said. "I'm the law in Santa Fe."

"Then arrest this man for murder while he's still alive," Houston ordered.

"Sheriff," Pritchard said, relaxing, "I can explain. The prisoner tried to escape and—"

Whatever else Pritchard was about to say was cut short as Houston crossed the small office in three swift strides.

Pritchard went for his gun, but he was a second too late. Houston's first punch, a thunderous uppercut, lifted the deputy completely off the ground, slamming his head against the cell. Houston's second punch was like the driving piston of a steam locomotive as it struck Pritchard right where his ribs connected below his breastbone.

When she was twelve, Dixie had accidentally been elbowed in the solar plexus while wrestling with Ruff. She still remembered the paralyzing pain, and now she saw it reflected on Pritchard's face as he turned fish-belly white and tried to breathe. Before Pritchard could even moan, Houston's overhand right landed in the middle of his face, and everyone in the office heard Pritchard's nose snap like a dried stick.

The next three or four seconds were an exhibition of unleashed fury the likes of which Dixie hoped never to see again. Before the sheriff and the other deputy could grab Houston and pull him off Pritchard, no less than five more savage blows were administered, as Houston's fists turned the deputy's face to mush.

Pritchard was out on his feet, his coat hooked on the cell bars, his body twitching on bent knees. Houston struggled for a moment, then lowered his fists. He slowly turned around, and the sheriff and the deputy retreated.

Houston said, "Your deputy hit my sister and he murdered his prisoner. What are you going to do about it?"

The sheriff, a middle-aged man with pale blue eyes and jowls, stammered, "If he lives, we'll try him for murder."

Houston lowered his bloody knuckles. "Fair enough," he breathed, heading for the door.

If anything, the crowd outside had grown larger. Dixie and Houston paid them no mind as they remounted their Thoroughbreds and drove them through the people and then on up the streets of Santa Fe, heading off to find Ruff and Marshal Gus.

It was only after they were several miles out of town that they pulled their horses in and Dixie looked closely at her brother, whose face was a brittle mask. "Houston, are you all right?"

"I am," he said. "I didn't kill the man. Are you satisfied?"

"I am," Dixie repeated in a small voice.

NINETEEN

"Marshal Gus, I still don't think this is going to work," Ruff complained as he watched the marshal dress himself in the part of a ragged miner with a floppy hat, round-toed shoes, and tattered suspenders.

"Why not?"

"Because you just don't look like a miner."

"Aw, what the hell do you know?" Gus groused. "You came from Tennessee! Ain't nothing but a bunch of farmers and cotton pickers live there."

"It's true that I haven't seen a lot of miners," he admitted, "but I've never seen a . . ."

"A what?" Gus demanded.

"A fat one," Ruff blurted. "Miners are always lean and muscular because they work so hard."

Gus's cheeks blew out and he looked ready to kill, but somehow he managed to contain himself. "Look," he explained, "all we got to do is to get the drop on Laredo and his pack of ambushers. My trousers are so baggy that I can slip my shotgun right down my leg and whip the damned thing out when we get the drop on 'em. After that, you just stay outa my way and let me and my shotgun do the talking."

"Whatever you say," Ruff agreed, knowing that Gus would do no such thing.

"I'll just state my name and authority and tell 'em to raise their damned hands," the marshal said, thinking out loud.

"I won't just blast them to Kingdom Come the way they deserve."

"That's fine, but do you really think that Laredo and his friends will let us arrest them and escort them back to Rio Paso for a certain necktie party?"

"Probably not," the marshal admitted, "but either way we get to split a big reward. Be easier if I need to kill this Laredo fella. As for the others, we'll just see which way the wind blows."

"Fair enough," Ruff said without any confidence at all.

"But you're sure they were the ones that ambushed our boys up near Little Alder Creek?"

"No question about that," Ruff said. "After I finally got them to let me join them at the poker table, a couple of 'em said things that left no doubt in my mind. I could tell that Laredo didn't like their loose talk, but he didn't say anything or even seem the least bit worried."

"He probably figures that in Cyclone, anybody can get away with any damn thing, including murder. And there's the matter of Charlie Benson's Stetson with its rattlesnake-skin hatband."

"Yes," Ruff said. "The fella named Yoder is wearing it, and there is no doubt it's the hat that you've described."

"All right then," Gus said, reaching down for a handful of dirt and rubbing it on his face, then his thick arms. "Do I look earthy enough to be a miner now?"

"Dirty enough, sure, but not skinny enough."

"To hell with skinny," Gus said, reaching for his shotgun and easing it down one pant leg.

"How's it feel?" Ruff asked, with an amused smile.

"It feels like if it went off by accident, I would be able to sing like a canary." The sheriff buttoned a ragged coat over his worn and dirty shirt. "There, can you see it now?"

Ruff laughed outright and studied the marshal's leg where the bulge of the shotgun's barrel was clearly evident. "Gus, it does look like you have some kind of physical abnormality. But other than that, I think you're fine."

Gus unbuttoned his coat and hurled it to the ground. "That coat is crawlin' with lice! Couldn't you have gotten a better one?"

"Not for two bits."

Gus shivered with revulsion, and after he had carefully removed the shotgun, he began to scratch vigorously. "I sure wish you'd have gotten some better clothes."

"Besides being cheap, they were the only ones that I could find that would fit you," Ruff said pointedly. "Now, quit complaining and start walking."

"I could ride to the edge of town and then—"

"No," Ruff said with finality. "You're a miner now. A down-at-the-heels and dead-broke miner. That being the case, you wouldn't have a horse."

"Yeah, but—"

"You've had almost a week to do nothing but rest while I've been trying to get in good with Laredo and his friends. I've done my part, Gus. Now it is time to do yours."

"You're a hard, hard man, Rufus Ballou."

"I'm a man who wants to get this whole thing over with and get back to my sister and our horses."

Marshal Gus looked up at the dying sun. "Then let's settle this thing tonight."

"Suits me just fine," Ruff said, going to saddle the sheriff's horse. "I'll leave High Fire hidden in those willows just over yonder."

"Why?"

"Just in case we step into a hornet's nest and there is nothing to do but run or get stung to death."

The marshal started to say something, but then he changed his mind and dipped his chin in agreement. "If I should go down, you send my share of the reward to my girls. Understand?"

"Sure, and if the same thing happens to me, don't forget that my share goes to my sister, as does that stallion."

"I ain't likely to forget," Gus said, still scratching.

Ruff stepped into the now familiar saloon where 'he'd spent every evening of the last week-and-a-half. The bartender who had harangued him so badly that first night had finally gotten friendly. His name was Cassidy, and he was fiercely protective of his rough clientele.

"The usual?"

Ruff nodded. He was glad that this was the last night he would be playing this game because he was about flat broke even though he'd been trying to conserve the last of his money.

"You find any work yet?" Cassidy asked.

"Nothing," Ruff replied.

"It's tough. Be two bits."

Ruff paid and tried to relax. He was not carrying his rifle around anymore, and his pistol was stuffed under his waistband. He knew that in a very short while, Laredo and his friends would start to drift into the saloon, and then Marshal Gus, probably tired, thirsty, and footsore, would come limping in to make the arrest.

Ruff spent the next hour nursing two beers. When Laredo and his friends arrived, he nodded a greeting to them.

Laredo said, "Hey, you got money to lose again tonight?"

"Nope," Ruff said, trying to smile. "You and your friends about won the last of it."

"Too bad," Laredo said without sympathy. "You're too damn young to be playing poker with men."

Ruff bit back a response. He wasn't at all too young, and he resented like hell the inference. What he'd done was to lose a little money deliberately so that he could look green, inexperienced, and, therefore, pose no threat.

Laredo took his customary seat that positioned his back to the wall. Ruff ordered a third beer as more customers wandered in. When Marshal Gus finally arrived, he looked surprisingly authentic. He also looked footsore and ferocious.

"Whiskey," he ordered, limping up the bar to stand near Ruff, who wondered if the limp was genuine, or if it was just because the marshal had that shotgun running halfway down his thigh.

Cassidy poured Gus a beer. "New in town, ain't ya?"

"I am."

"Looking for work?"

"Not in a flea-trap saloon like this one."

Cassidy bristled. "Mister, from the looks of you, I'd say you'd take about any work that was offered, including cleaning my spittoons."

Gus's hand shot across the plank bar, and he grabbed Cassidy's wrist and crunched it so hard that the bartender grew pale. "Now," Gus said, "I guess you had just better keep your damned opinions to yourself."

Cassidy, lips drawn back in a painful grimace, nodded rapidly. Satisfied, Gus released the man, looking pleased with himself.

But Ruff was anything but pleased, because Laredo and his friends were eyeing Gus very closely. Especially Laredo.

"Cassidy is our friend," Laredo drawled. "And I think you'd better apologize right now, fat man."

"And I think you can just kiss my big behind!"

Ruff groaned. This was hardly the way to get the drop on these hardcases.

Laredo came to his feet, knocking his chair backward, hand shading his gun butt. "Mister," he said, "I don't know and I don't care if you are packing a gun, but you had better fall to your knees and beg for your life or I will personally ventilate your gizzard."

When Gus darkened with rage, the other men at the table also came to their feet. Ruff slid down the bar until he was out of the line of fire, and his own hand inched closer to his gun.

"Well?" Laredo asked. "What's it going to be, fat man?"

There was no way that Gus could draw that big shotgun out of his pants and beat Laredo and his friends to the draw, so Ruff figured he had better stage a distraction.

"Excuse me?"

Laredo glanced sideways at him. "What do you want?"

"I changed my mind about playing cards," Ruff blurted.

"Huh?"

"I changed my mind," Ruff said. "Look!"

Laredo *did* look, and that's when Ruff drew his six-gun and caught them all off guard.

"What the—"

Laredo didn't finish whatever he'd meant to say because the man beside him went for his gun. Ruff shot the ambusher in the chest, and in that split second of confusion, Gus managed to get his shotgun out of his pants and pull one of his two triggers. The effect was devastating. Three ambushers were knocked over backward, and Laredo dove for the floor, his own gun coming up spitting lead.

Ruff fired twice, and Laredo took both bullets through the neck and shoulder. He tried to raise his six-gun, but Ruff shot him through the head. Gus's second barrel cleared the room. One ambusher was struck so violently that he crashed through the wall, dead before he landed in the alley.

Gus, smoking shotgun in hand, stood up grinning and then began to scratch. "I guess we did it the easy way, huh, Ruff?"

Ruff started to speak, but then he gaped because Cassidy drew a pistol and shoved it into the marshal's ear.

"Move an inch and you're dead, mister. And you over there, drop that pistol or your friend's brains will decorate my walls."

Ruff dropped his gun because it was empty anyhow.

"I'm the marshal of Rio Paso," Gus said out of the corner of his mouth to the bartender. "And those men were bank robbers and ambushers."

"Too bad," Cassidy hissed. "Because they were also my friends. And for that, you're both going to pay."

Ruff didn't know what that might mean, but he had a bad feeling he was going to find out.

TWENTY

"What they hell are you going to do with us!" Gus demanded.

"You're both about to find out," the bartender said as he prodded them into the street and yelled, "Boys, we got us the marshal of Rio Paso and his deputy."

Men were already pouring out of the saloons to see what all the shooting was about.

"What in blazes happened in your place?" a bearded man shouted. "Sounded like a war."

"Not quite," Cassidy said, lips drawn back. "But the marshal and his young friend did manage to get the drop on Laredo and his men. Shot 'em all down in cold blood."

"That's not true!" Ruff challenged. "Besides, those men ambushed a posse."

This announcement brought cheers, and that told Ruff that he and Gus were in serious trouble.

"Let's string 'em up to that big oak tree just like the last lawmen we caught in Cyclone!" another man yelled.

Ruff looked sideways at Gus, and damned if the old lawman wasn't smiling.

"Do you find something about this that is amusing?" Ruff snapped in anger.

Marshal Gus leaned close and whispered, "Just between you and me, I think they're bluffing."

"Bluffing?" Ruff studied the hard and excited faces of the men of Cyclone. "Gus, if I didn't know better, I'd swear you were drunk."

"Don't worry, they'll come to their senses."

"Before or after we hang?"

Gus chuckled. "Just don't panic."

Ruff was trying not to panic, but the sheriff didn't seem to understand their desperate circumstances. Two ropes were found, and each already was formed into a hangman's noose, which gave Ruff something dark to consider.

"Let's go!" Cassidy shouted, as other men prodded them forward. The crowd cheered, acting like this was to be a celebration.

"What are we going to do?" Ruff hissed.

"I'm thinking."

"Think fast because there's the hanging tree!"

It was a big, wild oak at the end of the town, with twisted branches as thick as the barrel of a horse. The mob was excited, and when they reached the oak, both ropes were hurled over a monstrous branch and the nooses were dropped over Ruff's and Gus's throats.

"Have you thought of anything yet!" Ruff choked, sweat oozing from every pore.

"Yep."

"You have?"

"Yep!"

Marshal Gus cleared his throat. "Boys, you can hang us and it'll be entertainment for about two minutes."

"Damned good entertainment!" a drunken miner shouted.

"Or," Gus said, voice overriding the cheers, "you can collect the rich reward that our town has put up, getting even with Laredo and his bunch of ambushers."

"How much was the reward?"

"A thousand dollars," Gus shouted. "And all you got to do is to help us deliver their bodies to Rio Paso."

"Don't listen to them!" Cassidy shouted. "What makes you think that they'll pay you anything once they are safe in Rio Paso!"

A lively discussion ensued, during which time Ruff thought he might well be breathing his last. But the lure of big money was stronger than the lure of two minutes' lively entertainment.

"Will you swear on your honor that we'll have the reward!" a miner demanded to know. " 'Cause if you try to double-cross us, we'll burn Rio Paso to the ground!"

"And they'd do it, too," Ruff said under his breath.

"I know," Gus replied. "All right! A thousand dollars and you got my word on it!"

"Don't believe them!" Cassidy shouted.

"Offer them the whole damned twenty-five hundred, for God's sake!" Ruff choked.

"Shhh!" Gus hissed. "I'll be damned if we've gone through all this hell for nothing! Now, shut up, boy!"

"Marshal Gus is a man of his word. Ain't that right, Gus?" a man in the crowd yelled.

"You bet I am!"

Ruff was actually starting to breathe easier when suddenly everyone heard the hoofbeats of running horses, and then Elias Benson and his cowboys emerged at a hard gallop up the street. When the old man saw Gus standing bareheaded with a noose around his neck, Elias cursed and spurred his horse into the mob.

Men scattered rather than be trampled, and when Elias grabbed the end of the rope and forced his horse past, he tried to dally the rope around his saddle horn and break Gus's neck.

But Gus was too quick. Although fat and past his prime, he simply rooted his heels into the dirt, and when Benson's horse struck the end of the rope, Elias's fingers were crushed between the rope and his saddle horn. The old man shrieked with pain and wheeled his horse around, drawing his six-gun.

"I'll kill you!" Elias screamed as he tried to run Gus into the earth.

"You crazy old coot!" Gus hollered, jumping aside and flipping the hangman's rope up and over Elias, then backpedaling like crazy.

When the vengeance-filled rancher and his horse struck the end of the rope a second time, Elias was torn from his saddle. He struck the ground rolling. Gus was on him in a heartbeat, and one chopping blow at the base of Elias's neck was enough to put that hate-filled old man to sleep. Gus hog-tied the rancher while Ruff snatched Elias's gun.

"Party is over," Ruff told the rancher's cowboys. "Ride back to where you came from."

"But what about the boss?"

"You can visit him in jail," Gus replied. "Now, git!"

An hour later, a wagon was hitched and ready to roll. In the back of it lay Elias Benson, gagged and madder than a teased badger. Alongside of him lay the bodies of Laredo and his ambushers. And beside the wagon, on horses and on foot, came an army of miners and assorted riffraff, all determined to get their ten or twenty dollars of the reward.

"Seven hundred and fifty dollars each," Gus whispered, looking very pleased with himself.

"Shut up," Ruff ordered, still unable to believe that they had escaped being hanged while making money.

It was quite a procession they made as they rode and marched north, and it must have made quite an impression on Dixie and Houston, because they were both speechless, something of a rarity in either case.

"Howdy, brother," Ruff called, "welcome back to the family!"

Houston galloped up to grab Ruff around the shoulders and give him a hard, brotherly hug. "What the hell is going on here?"

"It's kind of a long story," Ruff said with a wink. "And one that I'd better explain later."

Dixie and Houston exchanged glances and seemed to understand that this was no time to go into details.

Ruff reached out and slapped his brother on the shoulder. "The only thing that really matters is that our family is together again."

"That reward matters," Houston said. "The way I understand it, we're horse poor and cash broke."

"All in good time, Houston," Ruff assured his long lost brother, "the money will all come in good time."

Dixie didn't know what was going on, but right now her tall Tennessee brothers looked so happy and fine on their Ballou stallions that even money didn't seem to matter.

WESTERNS!

NO OBLIGATION

Mail the coupon below

To start your subscription and receive 2 FREE WESTERNS, fill out the coupon below and mail it today. We'll send your first shipment which includes 2 FREE BOOKS as soon as we receive it.

Mail To: **True Value Home Subscription Services, Inc. P.O. Box 5235**
120 Brighton Road, Clifton, New Jersey 07015-5235

YES! I want to start reviewing the very best Westerns being published today. Send me my first shipment of 6 Westerns for me to preview FREE for 10 days. If I decide to keep them, I'll pay for just 4 of the books at the low subscriber price of $2 75 each; a total $11.00 (a $21.00 value). Then each month I'll receive the 6 newest and best Westerns to preview Free for 10 days. If I'm not satisfied I may return them within 10 days and owe nothing. Otherwise I'll be billed at the special low subscriber rate of $2.75 each; a total of $16.50 (at least a $21.00 value) and save $4.50 off the publishers price. There are never any shipping, handling or other hidden charges. I understand I am under no obligation to purchase any number of books and I can cancel my subscription at any time, no questions asked. In any case the 2 FREE books are mine to keep.

Name
_____

Street Address _____ Apt. No. _____

City _____ State _____ Zip Code _____

Telephone _____

Signature _____
(if under 18 parent or guardian must sign)

Terms and prices subject to change. Orders subject
to acceptance by True Value Home Subscription
Services Inc

11434-0